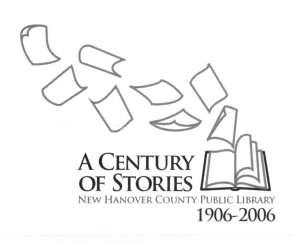

A CENTURY
OF STORIES
NEW HANOVER COUNTY PUBLIC LIBRARY
1906-2006

Sarah's Song

**Center Point
Large Print**

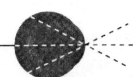

**This Large Print Book carries the
Seal of Approval of N.A.V.H.**

KAREN KINGSBURY

CENTER POINT PUBLISHING
THORNDIKE, MAINE

This Center Point Large Print edition
is published in the year 2005 by arrangement with
Warner Faith, a division of Time Warner Book Group.

The text of this Large Print edition is unabridged. In other
aspects, this book may vary from the original edition. Printed in
Thailand. Set in 16-point Times New Roman type.

ISBN 1-58547-537-8

Library of Congress Cataloging-in-Publication Data

Kingsbury, Karen.
    Sarah's song / Karen Kingsbury.--Center Point large print ed.
        p. cm.
    ISBN 1-58547-537-8 (lib. bdg. : alk. paper)
      1. Older women--Fiction. 2. Nursing students--Fiction. 3. Female friendship--Fiction.
    4. Nursing home patients--Fiction. 5. Reminiscing in old age--Fiction. 6. Large type books.
    I. Title.

PS3561.I4873S27 2005
813'.54--dc22
                                                                                    2004016853

To Donald, my prince charming—you know the words to my song and sing it with me whenever I forget.

To Kelsey, my only daughter—your heart is laced together with mine; I feel it even when I'm a world away.

To Tyler, my music lover—you dream of Broadway and sing the soundtrack in the fairy tale that is our life.

To Sean, my tender boy—look over your shoulder at how far you've come, and try to imagine the rainbows ahead.

To Josh, my gentle giant—your strength is surpassed only by your ability to love. How glad I am that God gave you to us.

To EJ, my wide-eyed wonder—you are becoming everything we knew you could be; the sunbeam of your life keeps me warm on the coldest days.

To Austin, my miracle boy—your every heartbeat is testimony to God's grace and mercy. I see your fist raised to the sky after a soccer goal, and I can only think that somewhere in heaven the angels are doing the same thing.

And to God Almighty, who has—for now—blessed me with these.

Sarah's Song

It's not too late for faith to find us.
Not too late for right to win.
Not too late, let love remind us.
Not too late to try again.

In my life the straight and narrow had a face, and it
*   was yours.*
I took crooked paths around you, shut you out, and
*   locked the doors.*
Long I wandered tired and aimless, seeking all the
*   world might hold.*
There you waited, true and blameless, soul of good-
*   ness, heart of gold.*

Nothing lasting came of those days, months of bitter
*   freezing rain.*
I was blinded, couldn't see you, choosing sorrow,
*   living pain.*
Then one day I looked behind me, at the way life
*   could've been.*
Suddenly I had to find you, had to see your face again.

Somewhere in my mind I see a place for me and you.
A place where faith might find a future, give us both a
*   life brand new.*
Together in God's mighty grip is where we both
*   belong.*

Find me, know me, teach your heart the words to Sarah's Song.

It's not too late for faith to find us.
Not too late for right to win.
Not too late for love to bind us.
Not too late to try again.

Sarah's Song

PROLOGUE

THE RITUAL WAS SACRED, drawn out for twelve days, the same every Christmas.

Sarah Lindeman looked out the smudged window of her cramped room at Greer Retirement Village, and already she could hear the music, feel her tired, old vocal chords coming together to sing again. The way they came together every thirteenth of December.

The box was opened, its contents spread across the worn bedspread. Twelve envelopes, yellowed and faded by the years, the way all of life was faded now. All except the memory of that single year, the year when heaven cracked open and spilled stardust and miracles into the life of a young woman who had given up hope.

She was that girl, and the year was 1941.

Patched together, the events of that time created a journey, a story she remembered still, every teardrop and smile, every exchange of words, every bit of laughter. Every impossible twist and turn down the alleys of a yesterday even time couldn't touch.

Sarah had broken the story into twelve parts, created twelve paper ornaments, each with a single word or words to remind her. Over the years it became the ritual it was today. Twelve ornaments, one each for the twelve days of Christmas, a chance each December to drift back through the decades, back to 1941, and remember it all again.

And there was the song, of course, playing in the background, standing like an anthem for all they'd known, all she missed now that he was gone. The notes, the melody, the haunting refrains pulled from the story of their lives. Always she would sing the song. She would hum it at first, and then as the days of December wore on, the words would come. They would come as they had at the beginning, born of despair, desperate for a second chance.

All of it, every word, every note, for Sam.

Sarah turned around, leaned hard into her aluminum walker, and shuffled to the bed. Distant voices filled the hallway outside her room, staff assistants talking to the elderly residents the way young people did these days, loud and condescending; someone going on about the cooking staff and its bland version of lasagna.

And somewhere above it all the piped-in refrains of "Silent Night."

Sarah eased herself down next to the envelopes. The bed seemed lower all the time. Her hips hurt worse this year, and each breath came slower, with more effort. No doubt her time was short. Death wasn't far off.

Not that Sarah minded. Dying, after all, would reunite her with Sam.

Had it been thirteen years since his death? Thirteen years since she'd shared this Christmas ritual with the man who had made it possible? Back then they'd gone through the twelve days together—taking out the ornaments, finding their way through the days and months and years back to 1941, remembering their story.

Singing the song.

She was eighty-six now, and if Sam had lived he'd be ninety-one. Instead, cancer had taken him—not slowly over a course of years, but in six months. That May he was traveling with her to Los Angeles to see the kids, to welcome the birth of a great-granddaughter. A sluggish few weeks, a bad blood test, and he was gone before Thanksgiving.

At first Sarah lived alone in the old house where they'd raised their two children and entertained grandchildren. The house was as much a part of the glorious past as anything else because it was walking distance to the park, the place where it had all come together.

But more years passed and she grew tired, too tired to dress in the morning or take a walk or shop for groceries. Heart failure, the doctor told her. Nothing imminent, just a slow and steady decline that would worsen over time.

After her diagnosis, the kids had taken a week off work and tried to talk her into moving to LA. Sarah was gracious, glad for their concern, but only one place could possibly serve as her final home, the place where she would live out her days.

The facility was built across from the park the summer after Sam died. Greer Retirement Village. Assisted living, they called it. An oversized bedroom with space enough for a recliner and television. Also a kitchenette with a sink, a microwave, and small refrigerator. The staff organized bingo on Tuesdays,

Bible study on Wednesdays, low-impact aerobics on Thursdays, and old movies on Fridays. Meals were served on china and linen twice a day in the dining room, and on weekends they had live entertainment in the form of Mr. Johnson, the assistant manager who also played the piano.

Most of all, each room had emergency buttons near the bed and in the bathroom, and staff assistants who came by to remind residents about their medication—how much and when to take it.

And so, after a few days' discussion, the kids had come around and reserved Sarah a place at the village. A room on the first floor overlooking the park and the bench. The very same bench where Sarah had written the song in the first place.

"I'll never leave," she told the kids before they returned to LA. "This—" She waved toward the window and the park and the bench beyond. "—is where I'll feel your father every day." She hesitated. "I'll come see you; don't worry."

They understood, both Harry who was fifty-five that year, and Sharon, fifty-three. And at first Sarah kept her promise, heading for California two weeks each summer and two weeks in January. But her heart failure progressed, and three years back the doctor ordered her to stop flying. Sarah was moved to the third floor, to a wing that was more nursing home than assisted living.

But she kept her view of the park bench.

And she kept the ritual, the twelve days of Christmas.

Sarah rested her weathered fingers on the first envelope and a thrill worked its way through her. The story always did that to her, always moved her heart a few inches closer to her throat and made her mouth dry. No matter how many decades had passed, the memory of that year made her feel young and in love and awed by the miracle they'd shared.

She dusted her fingertips over the old envelopes one at a time, the numbers scrawled across the fronts reminding her, filling her spirit, readying her soul for the remembering that was to come. If this was the last time, the last Christmas, then she'd need a little help.

Her eyes narrowed and she lifted her face toward the window. "Dear God . . ." The words were a scratchy whisper. "Make the days come to life again, every moment. Please."

The quiet prayer hung in the room for a moment, and then slowly a thought began to form. If this was the last time she was going to remember, the last time she would sing her song, then someone had to hear it. Not just hear it but feel it—feel it in the fabric of their heart the way Sarah did.

God had promised her that much, hadn't He?

A stranger needing encouragement, a doctor or a nurse, one of the staff assistants. Someone at Greer Retirement Village who would be changed by "Sarah's Song," the way she had been changed by it so long ago. She cleared her throat and struggled to her feet again. The walker seemed lighter, her bones filled with an energy that came every December. When she reached the window, with a clear view of the park bench, she finished her prayer.

"Send someone, God. Someone who needs hope." She could feel her eyes dancing despite the cataracts that clouded them. "Someone who could learn the song."

When she finished praying, a certainty filled her and made her long for tomorrow, the first of the twelve days. Something different was going to happen this time; she could feel it in her soul.

Now all she had to do was wait.

CHAPTER ONE

DECEMBER 13 DAWNED bright and sunny, unseasonably warm according to the morning nurse. Sarah didn't mind. Temperatures in South Carolina could change in an afternoon, and snow wasn't out of the question. Even for the week ahead. Snow had been a part of their first December; it was bound to come sometime in the next twelve days.

Beth Baldwin was in charge that morning. Beth was a young caregiver who never spoke more than the essentials. *Good morning. How are you? Nice December we're having.* That sort of thing. Beth was married, or at least Sarah suspected as much since Beth wore a wedding ring. She was a pretty girl, a gentle caregiver, but her eyes were wild and restless. They reminded Sarah of something she couldn't quite take hold of.

"Beth, dear, do you know what day it is?" Sarah leaned forward so Beth could ease her into her red Christmas sweater.

The young woman blew a wisp of dark hair off her forehead. Her voice was pleasant, but she didn't make eye contact. "Monday, December 13."

A soft chuckle came from Sarah's throat. "No, dear. I don't mean the date, I mean the day." Sarah waited until she had Beth's attention.

"The day?" Beth straightened, one hand on her hip. "I give up; what's special about today?"

"Why, it's the First Day of Christmas!"

Beth cocked her head. "You mean like the song? The partridge in a pear tree and all that Twelve Days of Christmas stuff?"

"Yes." Sarah tugged on the sides of her sweater, and when it lay smooth around her scant frame, she eased back against the pillow. "Today's the first day."

"Hmmm." Beth took hold of the water pitcher sitting on Sarah's bedside table. "I thought those were the twelve days after Christmas."

"Only in the history books, dear. My twelve days begin today."

"Oh." Beth stopped. "Okay. That's nice I guess." With purposeful steps, she went to the sink, rinsed the pitcher, filled it, and returned it to its place. "I guess that means one thing." She stopped and gave Sarah a lopsided smile. "Twelve shopping days until Christmas."

Sarah pursed her lips, the prayer from last night playing over in her mind. Beth wasn't the one; she wouldn't hold a conversation, never mind listen to a story that stretched over twelve days.

"You know the routine." Beth headed for the door with a glance over her shoulder. "Press the call button if you need anything."

"Thank you, Beth. I'll be okay for a few—"

She was gone. Sarah stared at the closed door and gave a gentle shrug of her shoulders. Just as well. If Beth wasn't the one she'd prayed for, better to be alone for the first day of the ritual. She'd been waiting for this moment since the leaves began turning orange back in October.

The envelopes lay fanned out on her nightstand in numerical order, the small plastic tree set up a few inches away, pressed against the wall. Sarah shifted to that side of the bed and let her legs hang over the side until her woolly socks rested on the cold linoleum floor.

The first envelope called out to her, begging to be opened. She lifted the flap, removed the paper ornament, and studied the word scrawled across both sides.

Tomorrow.

That's what she had wanted that cold January day, wasn't it? Everything about tomorrow. Today, what she had in the moment, was never enough. Not Greer or her parents or their faith. Not even Sam. Everything she'd done back then was focused on tomorrow, that far-off day when she could go after everything country music had to offer. Everything a young woman with her looks and voice and determination deserved. Everything her small town of Greer couldn't offer. Every moment of it.

Tomorrow.

Sarah studied the word, the faded ink, and bit by bit the piped-in music, the conversations in the hall, the aches and pains of nearly nine decades, all grew dim. She closed her eyes, and in a rush she felt herself going back, pulled into a time that still existed, a time that had never really ended at all. She blinked her eyes open, and she was no longer perched on the edge of her bed at Greer Retirement Village.

She was twenty-three, in her parents' farmhouse across the street from the high school. Her mother was canning in the kitchen and the smell of warm apples and cinnamon filled the air. It was Christmas Eve 1940, and Sam Lindeman was over. The way Sam always had been back then.

Sarah fingered the paper ornament in her hand and blinked. She felt the weathered skin above her eyebrows bunch up and she pulled herself from the memory. She couldn't start in 1940. No, she had to go back to her girlhood days, when she dreamed day and night of catching Sam's attention, dating him, and one day marrying him.

Sam was five years older than she, the brother of Sarah's best friend, Mary. Though the Lindemans sometimes vacationed with Sarah's family, Sam never noticed Sarah in the early years. His age stood like an ocean, the span of time too far to consider bridging. But sometime after her twelfth birthday, despite their age difference, Sarah fell hard for him.

"He's so cute," she would tell Mary whenever the two were visiting. Back then, they spent hours listening to records in Mary's room, pretending they were famous singers.

"Nah," Mary would wrinkle her nose and turn up the music. "He's just my bossy brother."

Sam played football for Greer High and Sarah used to dream of aging four years overnight, waking one morning, showing up at the high school, and being Sam Lindeman's girl. They would graduate high school and head for some foreign land—Spain, maybe, or the South of France or the Bahamas. One of the places her teachers were always talking about.

In the dream, Sam would lead tourists on daring excursions and she would gain fame and fortune singing—not in a church choir the way her mother wanted her to sing, but in fancy dance halls and night-clubs, decked in beautiful gowns, with Sam sitting in the front row smiling at her.

The dream never panned out. Every morning Sarah woke up still twelve years old, and the next year Sam graduated from high school and went off to college without so much as a good-bye to his kid sister's little friend.

Years passed, and Sarah kept singing. By the time she turned seventeen everyone in Greer knew about her gift.

She'd been born with a voice that could silence a room; a voice her mama said would make angels cry with envy. Sarah proved it again and again, every Sunday when the church choir featured her as a soloist. Each week Sarah smiled and sang her heart out. But she hated singing in a choir robe. She kept a small calendar beneath her bed where she counted down the days until she could finish high school and take her singing somewhere exciting—Nashville or New York or Chicago. Anywhere but Greer.

One summer Sam returned home for an entire month. Four years had passed since Sam left for college, and he no longer figured into Sarah's dreams. Sarah would never forget the first time she saw him that July day. That morning at the Lindeman house, she was on her way up the stairs to find Mary when she heard a man's voice call to her from the dining room.

She turned and there he was. Sam Lindeman, twenty-two years old, taller, more filled out and more handsome than she had remembered. Sarah's breath caught in her throat and she froze near the bottom of the stairs. Visions of Spain and France and the Bahamas flashed in her mind.

"Sarah, look at you." He crossed the parlor to the place where she stood. His voice fell a notch and his eyes seemed to find her for the first time. "What happened to the little girl down the street?"

"Uh . . ." Heat rushed into Sarah's cheeks and she remembered to smile. "I grew up." She batted her eyelashes, willing herself to exhale.

"I guess so." He leaned against the wall, watching her. "You must be, what, seventeen now?"

"Yes." She was breathing again, but her racing heart threatened to give her away. "I'll be a senior in the fall."

"You're beautiful. I almost didn't recognize you."

"Gosh," Sarah lowered her chin, suddenly shy. "Thanks. I mean . . . I guess we both grew up, huh?"

"Yeah." He was quiet for a moment, a smile playing at the corners of his lips. "Can I ask you something, little Sarah all grown up?"

She giggled and felt some of her confidence return. "Ask."

"I'm taking my sister out for burgers tonight." His

smile was as true as time, and her knees grew weak again. "Wanna come?"

Sarah didn't have to think about her answer. "Yes" was out of her mouth almost as soon as he finished asking. Her parents wouldn't mind; not if Mary was going along. Besides, Sarah chided herself, Sam wasn't interested in her. He was only being nice, probably wanting to catch up on the past four years.

That night they bowled before dinner and Sam entertained them with hilarious stories about his roommates back at college. Later, halfway through the meal, conversation turned to Sam's plans after college. Travel, Sarah expected him to say. Exploration and adventure and daring, the sort of life that long ago she had dreamed they'd share together.

Instead, he set his burger down and leaned forward. "I'm getting my teaching certificate and coming back home." His eyes held a new sort of knowing as they found hers. "I'll marry a local girl, raise a family; and teach in Greer. Be the principal one day." He shifted his attention back to his sister. "That's all I've ever wanted. Sooner the better." Once more he looked at her. "How about you, Sarah? What are you doing after high school?"

Sarah's head was still spinning from his answer. "I'm leaving Greer, getting a recording contract."

"Really?" His expression held a hint of amusement. "Someone told me you could sing."

"She's amazing." Mary ate a French fry and nodded hard. "One day everyone will know Sarah."

"That's the plan." Sarah tried to find an appropriate

laugh to help keep the conversation light, but none was available. Instead she excused herself.

Alone in the restroom she stared at the chipped mirror, her eyes wide. Marrying a local girl right out of college was one thing, but Sam Lindeman living and teaching in Greer? Forever in a town where the closest thing to entertainment was Al's Drive-In or family night at the library?

She shuddered and fear took a stab at her composure.

As a girl she'd dreamed of following Sam to the ends of the earth, and now that he was home, now that he'd finally noticed her, those feelings were coming to life again. But she never imagined the dream would take her no farther than the Greer city limit sign.

A mix of emotions competed for control inside her. She was in trouble. Not because of the way Sam had looked at her when he talked about his future, but because of the way her heart leapt within her when he did.

CHAPTER TWO

SARAH RAN HER THUMB over the first ornament and pressed her other hand into the small of her back. The first day of the Christmas ritual was always the longest.

Two years passed before she saw Sam Lindeman again.

This time it was August, and Sam found her working at The Mixer, a diner with cheap food, a jukebox, and more teenagers than tables. Sarah was delivering a platter of cheese pizza to a group of baseball players when Sam walked through the door. A booth full of girls looked his way and began whispering and giggling, trying to get his attention.

He ignored them, and from his spot near the door he searched until he found her. "Hi." The word was silent, mouthed as he held up one hand and gave her a brief wave.

She served the food, wiped her hands, and met him near the door. "Sam!" Without thinking, she stood on her toes and hugged him. "You're back."

"I did it, Sarah." He grinned. "You're looking at Jackson Elementary's new fourth-grade teacher."

A warning bell sounded on the panel of Sarah's heart, but she spoke too fast to heed it. "That's great, Sam!" She felt her eyebrows raise, and she clasped her hands, happy for him. "Mary didn't tell me you'd be home this soon."

His smile softened. "I thought you'd be gone. Off to find that recording contract."

The reminder stung. "I'm saving up the money. Then I'm going to Nashville." She lifted her chin, proud of her efforts. "I work seven days most weeks."

"Well," Sam's eyes met hers and held them. "If you can spare a night this weekend, I'd love to take you out."

"Really?" Sarah glanced at her tables, making sure none of her customers needed her. Butterflies rose and fell in her stomach. A date? With Sam Lindeman? She looked at him again, suddenly shy and soft spoken. "That'd be nice."

"Okay." He leaned in and kissed her on the cheek. "See you at six o'clock Saturday."

The days that followed were painfully slow.

"Is it a date?" her mother wanted to know before he showed up in his new Rambler. "Because I'm not sure a girl of nineteen should be seeing a man in his twenties."

"Mama, it's Sam. Our neighbor, remember? We used to vacation with them and you never worried."

In the end, her mother relented, agreeing that Sam couldn't possibly be a threat. Sarah had to laugh about her mama's reaction. Sam never wanted to leave Greer. If her mother had known that, she'd have Sarah married to him by Christmas.

Of course, regardless of what she told her mother, that first night definitely felt like a date. Sam brought her flowers, opened doors for her, and made her laugh so hard at one point she had tears streaming down her face. Before he walked her up the steps to her house that night, he turned and the two of them locked eyes. "I had fun tonight."

The summer temperatures had cooled and a strong breeze sifted over the front yard and up onto the porch. Sarah moved closer, so that only a few inches separated them. She was five-foot-seven, but he was still much taller than her. She held her breath. "Can I ask you something?"

He stuck his hands in his jeans pockets and the moonlight shone in his eyes. "Anything."

"Okay." She tilted her head, trying to figure him out. "Was this a date?"

His expression changed and slowly, a fraction of an inch at a time, he took hold of her hands and drew her close. Then, in the sweetest single moment of Sarah's life to that point, he kissed her. Sarah was dizzy with the feelings swirling inside her, glad she had Sam to lean against. Otherwise her knees wouldn't have held her up.

When they pulled apart, Sam searched her eyes. "Does that answer your question?"

Sarah had a dozen things to say, a hundred questions, but she let the most pressing rise to the top. "How long, Sam?" She exhaled, trying to catch her breath. "When did you stop seeing me as Mary's little friend?"

A sigh eased from Sam's lips. He released one of Sarah's hands and wove his fingers through her hair. "You wanna know?" He leaned in and kissed her again. "That morning when I saw you at the foot of our stairs. You were seventeen, and I thought I'd seen a vision. This blonde, blue-eyed angel walks through the front door and all of a sudden I realize it's you. Mary's friend, Sarah."

"But you didn't call." Sarah swallowed. Maybe she shouldn't be telling him this; maybe it would only make it harder to leave once she had the money to get away from Greer. "I thought . . ."

"I had school." He let his lips brush against her forehead, her cheekbones. "You had to grow up. But now, here we are." He drew back and gave her a crooked smile. "Maybe you're not supposed to leave Greer, Sarah. Ever think about that?"

She couldn't say anything. At that moment, all she wanted was to be lost in Sam's arms forever. Nothing could've pulled her from him. But later that night after he was gone, she reminded herself of the truth. No matter how much she enjoyed Sam's company, she had to move ahead with her plans. Leaving was something she'd spent a lifetime wanting, and not even Sam Lindeman could make her stay.

At least that was the idea.

In the end, Sarah did stay, for a while, anyway. For the next four years she dated Sam on and off. He took college courses toward his administrative credentials and hinted about marriage. She continued to sing at church, and without fail Sam sat in the second row, watching.

When Sam would call for a date, Sarah couldn't help but say yes. She loved him, didn't she? Besides, by then most of her friends were married and having babies. A night out with Sam was better than a night at home with her parents or an extra shift at The Mixer.

Every few months, Sarah counted her money and every few months she convinced herself she needed more if she wanted to do well in Nashville. In hindsight, she was only doing what was safe. Staying in Greer, dating the only man she'd ever desired, dreaming about a far-off future, but never actually packing her bags and making it happen.

Finally on Christmas Eve of 1940, Sam presented her with a ring. "Be my wife, Sarah." He dropped to one knee and the small diamond solitaire shone in the glow of the Christmas lights.

This was the part of the memory that matched most with the first ornament, the part that pained Sarah even now.

As if it had only just happened, Sarah could see herself. The way she stared at the ring as her head began to spin. How had she let their relationship get so serious? Why had it taken so long to save up the money to leave Greer, and how come she hadn't talked more often about her plans? There'd never been any question that she would leave as soon as she had the money.

Hadn't she made that clear?

With Sam still kneeling, still waiting for her answer, her words began tumbling out. "Sam, I'm sorry . . . I never . . ." She looked down, pinched the bridge of her nose, and gave a hard shake of her head. "I can't."

Slowly, as if he'd aged ten years in as many seconds, Sam stood. "Four years, Sarah." He hung his head so their foreheads touched. "You talked about moving away, but every month, every week you were still here. I thought . . ." He drew back and met her eyes. "I thought you stayed because of me; because you loved me."

"I do." She folded her arms tightly around her waist. "I care about you, Sam." Tears stung her eyes but she blinked them away. She hated the pain in his expression, hated the fact that she'd let him think she was ready to get married. "It's not about you. I have to get out of Greer. It'd kill me to stay here forever. I have to go, find a life outside of—"

"Stop." His voice was quiet, kind. "I understand." With that, Sam's expression changed once more. He no longer looked hurt and vulnerable, but resigned. He studied her for a long time, the desire from earlier that evening gone. In its place was the brotherly look he'd had for her back when she was a young girl. "It's over; no more explanation."

Sarah bit her lip, unable to stop the tears from spilling onto her cheeks. "I'm sorry, Sam."

"Shhh." He kissed her forehead. "Don't say it."

Then, without another word, he closed the small velvet ring box, slipped on his coat, and headed for the door. Before he left, his eyes met hers one last time and he whispered, "Good-bye, Sarah."

She watched him leave and over the next hour she packed her bags. She would go even if she didn't have enough money, go even if it meant never seeing Sam again. When the holidays were over, her parents drove her to the train station where she bid them good-bye, took hold of her two oversized suitcases—one of which held an envelope with every song she'd ever written—and boarded a passenger car that would make a handful of connections and eventually take her to Nashville.

The future lay out before her as the train pulled away. She was going to Nashville, going after the dream. She wanted more than a sweet, simple life with Sam Lindeman. She wanted a big stage and a packed house, a record contract and all the glitz and glamour that went with it. She didn't want a wedding and babies.

She wanted everything tomorrow had to offer.

And the entire train ride to Nashville she was absolutely convinced that's what she would find.

Sarah lowered the paper ornament to her lap.

Her back and legs were sore from sitting on the edge of the bed for so long. She closed her eyes against a wave of tears. The ritual was not without pain, especially at the beginning. How could she have walked away?

She sniffed hard and sat a bit straighter. Enough. She would take the pieces one at a time. Her eyes opened and despite her trembling fingers, she hung the ornament on one of the lower tree branches. Then she pulled her legs back onto the bed and rested against a mound of pillows. Her eyes moved across the tree—

only a few feet high, sparse and dime-store green—to the ornament.

Tomorrow indeed.

A long breath made its way through her clenched teeth and she looked toward the window. The song came next. Not the words, not until it was time. But the melody at least, the tune that had turned it all around. Notes forever etched in her mind.

The song couldn't come until she reached the window. Too tired to move just yet, she waited ten minutes, fifteen, twenty, until she was finally ready. Then, with a determination bigger than yesterday, she forced her legs over the edge, found her walker, and worked herself across the floor to the window. Ahh, yes. It was there still, and now that the twelve days had begun, she could almost see them, the two of them sitting there.

She and Sam.

The tune came, quietly at first and then louder until her humming filled the space around her. She leaned against the window and lowered her chin, searching the heavens, as the song rang out, trapped in her closed mouth. He was up there somewhere, her precious Sam. Could he see her now? Hear her?

The door opened behind her. "Sarah?"

She didn't turn. The song stopped for no one, because it couldn't. Sarah had to hum it all the way through before the first day would be complete. She hummed through the verse and the chorus. When it was over, she looked at the bench one last time and then turned around. "Yes?"

Beth had taken a seat at the end of Sarah's bed. "That was beautiful; someone told me you used to sing."

"Yes." Sarah smiled. The minutes spent in the past were never long enough. She pushed her walker back to the bed and allowed Beth to help her get under the covers.

"Did you sing professionally?" She tucked the sheet beneath Sarah's arms. Her tone was tinged with intrigue. "I mean, you know, did you record any- thing?"

Sarah considered the young caregiver and felt the corners of her lips lift. "I did." She leaned into the pil- lows. "It's a long story."

Beth looked around until her eyes fell on the small artificial tree. "Just one ornament?"

Sarah followed her gaze. "For now."

"Tomorrow." Beth narrowed her eyes and looked at Sarah. "Does it mean something?"

"Yes." Sarah folded her hands. "Much." She nodded to the envelopes spread across the nightstand at the foot of the tree. "One ornament for each of the twelve days of Christmas."

"I see." Beth smoothed out the wrinkles in the bed- spread. "Does each ornament have a word?"

"A word . . . and a story." Something warm ignited inside Sarah's soul. "Stay longer tomorrow. I'll tell you the story behind the second ornament. And after the twelfth day, I'll tell you the secret."

"The secret?" Beth raised an eyebrow, her expres- sion doubtful.

"The secret to love." Sarah managed a tired smile. "It's worth finding, Beth."

"Yes, well . . ." Beth gave a quiet nod, her eyes never leaving Sarah. "I might have to come back for something that special. The secret of love, and all."

Sarah bit her tongue. Beth thought she was a doddering old fool, eccentric and troubled by the ravages of old age. Nothing could be farther from the truth, but Sarah wouldn't say so. Beth would have to find out on her own.

The conversation ran out and Beth patted Sarah's hand. "Lunch'll be ready in a few minutes; just thought I'd warn you." She stood and headed for the door before stopping. "Sarah?"

"Yes?"

"Did you write the song, the one you were humming?"

"Yes." Sarah dropped her eyes and then looked at Beth again. "It's part of the story."

Beth nodded. "I thought so."

For a moment Sarah thought the young woman would ask more questions. But instead she reached for the door. "I'll get lunch."

The knowing came as soon as Beth left the room.

So she was the one after all. The one Sarah had prayed for. And God would bring her back. She would come tomorrow and hear the story, learn about the second ornament, find hope in the telling, even learn the words to the song.

And maybe, by the twelfth day, Beth would know it well enough to sing along.

CHAPTER THREE

THE SONG stayed with her.

Beth heard it in her head the entire drive home to Spartanburg. Sad, really, the old lady sitting in her room, singing some old song, reminding herself of a story that had been forgotten for decades.

The radio in Beth's Honda didn't work, so her mind wandered to the scene ahead. This was the night. Her planning and plotting and figuring out had finally come to this. She took one hand from the wheel and snagged a piece of gum from the side pocket of her purse. Without looking, she pushed the paper wrapping off, dropped it back into her purse, and popped the gum into her mouth.

Yes, tonight was the night.

She'd been talking with her mother about the separation for weeks, making promises that her time away from her husband would only be temporary. But she'd never told Bobby, never let on that the routine that passed for their marriage was making her crazy with boredom.

Bobby's face came to mind—simple, faithful, content. Uninteresting. How would he take the news? And what about their five-year-old daughter, Brianna? Beth pictured them, Bobby and Brianna. She would be watching TV with him now, same as every afternoon. Bobby worked maintenance at the local hospital, six to two. Brianna's preschool was on his way home.

What would happen to their routine after tonight? She squinted at the sun, bright and low in the sky. The good weather wouldn't last; not in December.

The song came to mind again.

Whatever the old lady's story, Beth was sure it involved a man. Sarah Lindeman might be pushing ninety, but she was a woman after all. And a woman in love couldn't hide the fact, nineteen or ninety-nine. It was that part that made Beth doubt she'd show up to hear the story. Not when she herself had spent a lifetime longing for that look, that kind of love.

Ahead of her, the two-lane road curved first right then left, and she saw her turn-off. The low-income neighborhood where they lived spread out for eight blocks, the houses small and old and boxy. But for the paint and a few differences in the trim, it was hard to tell one from another.

She wasn't a praying woman, but if she were, this would've been a good time to ask for help. She'd dropped out of college to marry Bobby Baldwin, and in seven years, the man had learned nothing about her. What she was about to do that night was sure to catch him off guard. She parked, grabbed her purse, and headed inside.

"Hello?" The screen door slammed behind her and she dropped her bag on the kitchen table. She turned and faced the sofa where Bobby and Brianna were watching television. Beth dropped to her knees and sat back on her heels. "Where's my Brianna bug?"

"Mommy!" Their little daughter bounced off Bobby's lap and ran across the room, honey-blonde ponytail flying behind her. "Guess what?"

"What?" Beth tried to sound excited. She nuzzled her face against Brianna's and kissed the tip of her nose.

"I made you a Cwis'mas present at school! And it was the bestest one in the whole class."

Beth smiled. "Do I get it now?"

"No," Brianna gave a hard shake of her head, her eyes serious. "Only on Cwis'mas morning."

"Okay." She looked over her daughter's shoulders at Bobby. "Tell you what, sweetie. You and Daddy can finish watching TV later."

Bobby cast her a curious look, but Beth ignored it. She stood and led Brianna down the hallway toward her bedroom. "How 'bout you go color a picture for Daddy, alright?"

Brianna gave a small gasp. Her eyes lit up, glowing with enthusiasm and innocence. "Okay, Mommy! Then I'll have a present for Daddy, too!"

"Yes, honey." Beth scooped her daughter up, held her for a minute, and walked her down the hall. "That would be very nice."

When Brianna was in her room, Beth headed back to Bobby. She could feel his eyes on her the moment she came into view, but she didn't look at him until she was seated at the other end of the sofa.

"Something wrong?" Only his eyes were directed at her; his body, his face were still locked on the TV. He still had the television remote in his hand.

Beth studied him, the tufts of brown hair sticking out of his old Braves baseball cap, the blue flannel shirt he'd worn every winter for the past five years. "Turn off the TV, Bobby." She crossed her arms. "We need to talk."

He clicked the remote and the television went dark. Then he shifted his body in her direction. "Okay." His crooked smile was still cute. It reminded her of the reasons she'd fallen for him in the first place. "What's up?"

Amazement washed over her. *Look at him,* she thought. *He doesn't have a clue what's coming.* She drew a deep breath and let the words come. "I'm leaving you, Bobby. Brianna and I are moving in with my mother."

Bobby waited a few seconds, then chuckled. "What's this? Some sort of Christmas joke?"

"No." Beth didn't blink. "I'm already packed."

The laughter in Bobby's eyes faded and his lower jaw fell open. "You're serious?"

"Yes."

A frustrated anger filled his face. "Don't be crazy, Beth. We haven't fought in a month and now you're walking out on me? At Christmastime?" He let his head fall back and forced out a mouthful of air. "Whatever's eating you, don't blame it on me, okay?" His eyes met hers. "Maybe you had a bad day. So . . . take a nap or a walk around the block. But don't threaten to leave, Beth. That isn't going to make things better."

Calm, Beth told herself. *Stay calm.* She had expected his reaction. Her voice was gentle, quieter than his. "Nothing's eating me, and I didn't have a bad day." She ran her tongue along her lower lip, searching for the words. "Look, Bobby, I've made up my mind. This—" She looked across the room and waved her hand at their cramped kitchen and then at him. "The way we live . . . you and me, none of it's the way it was supposed to turn out."

"Oh, I get it." Fire flashed in Bobby's eyes. He was a gentle man; Beth had only seen him angry a few times. Once, when she'd talked about wanting more from life, he'd thrown his guitar through the bedroom wall. She hoped this wouldn't be one of those nights. "There's someone else, right?"

She sighed and it came from the basement of her heart. "No. This isn't about anyone but me. I . . ." she lifted her shoulders. "I can't do this anymore."

He gave her a sarcastic nod. "Nice, Beth." He huffed. "What happened to the whole faith thing, living for God and doing things His way?" Bobby stood up and glared at her. "I thought marriages made in heaven didn't die. Weren't those your words?"

"Yes." She was ready for this, too. "I was young. We were both raised in the church, but so what? When's the last time you took us to a Sunday service? For that matter, when's the last time you took me any-where?"

"I don't need this, Beth." He gestured toward the hallway. "Brianna will hear you."

Beth didn't care. She stood up and kicked the sofa, her eyes boring into his. "Every night it's the same thing. You sit here watching that stupid television, and then you fall asleep before your head hits the pillow.

We don't laugh or talk or dance or date." She was louder than she meant to be. "I had dreams when I met you." A sound that was more cry than laugh came from her. "Now look at me. I can't take one more day of it, Bobby. Not one."

His mouth opened and for a moment it looked like he might shout at her. But then he gritted his teeth and looked away.

"You promised me more than this." She hesitated, and her voice lost some of its edge. "See. You can't deny it. What we have is meaningless—an existence, nothing more."

This time when he looked at her, the fight was gone. "Is that really how you see us?"

She sucked at the inside of her lip. "Yes." Her sniff punctuated the word. "I'm not in love with you, Bobby. I can't . . . I can't make myself feel something that isn't there. I need time. Me and Brianna will be at my mother's until I decide what to do next."

A slow disgusted shock colored his features. "Twelve days before Christmas, Beth? Couldn't you wait a few weeks? Give me a chance to make things right?"

"No!" She barely let him finish his sentence. Anxiety grabbed hold of her and shook hard. "I don't want to try again. It's not in you, Bobby. We've had this talk a dozen times. Things seem better for a week or two, but then they're right back the way they were." She spread her hands out. "This . . . this life we live is enough for you. Pretending for my sake won't turn things around. It never has before."

"Fine." Something hard as steel filled his eyes and he took a step back. "If you don't love me, I won't ask you to change your mind. But consider our daughter. Leaving now, a few weeks before Christmas? How do you think she'll feel about that?" He paused. "Wait two weeks for Brianna and then go." His lips were pinched as he spat out the last part. "I won't try to stop you."

Beth stood frozen in place, her mouth open.

What had he said? That he wouldn't try to stop her if she left after Christmas? That's what she wanted, wasn't it? It's what she'd wanted for two years. She'd expected to feel new and alive if Bobby released her, as if she'd been given a second lease on life. So, why didn't she feel better about it?

Instead her heart was heavy, and an emptiness made it hard for her to breathe.

She sat back down on the edge of the sofa. "Stay through Christmas?"

"Not for me." His look was harder than before. "For Brianna."

Beth swallowed. If she was going to leave, better to go now, right? Wasn't that what she'd decided when she made the plan? That way the holidays might take the edge off any sorrow Brianna would feel—sort of a softening of the blow.

But now, with the facts on the table, Bobby's argument made sense.

Staying home would at least give Brianna a happy Christmas, even if her parents were separating. They could keep the truth from her until the end of the month so that whatever pain Brianna felt, it wouldn't darken Christmas, too.

"Beth?" Bobby shifted his weight and flexed the muscles in his jaw.

"Okay." She looked at the ceiling. "I'll stay until the end of the month, but then we're gone."

"And until then?" Bobby looked away. His tone was so cold it made her shiver from across the room.

"Look . . ." She thought about fighting with him, then changed her mind. Her lungs emptied slowly, emphasizing her sadness. "I don't hate you. I just don't . . . I don't love you like I used to, Bobby. But Brianna doesn't have to know that." She hesitated. She hadn't counted on having to share a house with him even after he knew her feelings. "I think we need to be civil. Otherwise I can leave tonight."

"Civil?" His eyes found hers once more and this time, despite his obvious effort at indifference, the pain shone through. "Telling me two weeks before Christmas that you're walking out, Beth? Is that civil?"

They went another two rounds of her reasons and his explanations and promises, but it got them nowhere. In the end they agreed to keep their distance and focus their attention on their daughter. On giving Brianna a wonderful Christmas despite what the New Year would bring.

Beth kept to herself that evening. Sometime after nine o'clock she crept into Brianna's room and laid down on the floor. Sleep didn't find her at first. Instead a slideshow of pictures played in her mind.

Bobby and her on their first date; Bobby and her playing in the snow; Bobby and her teaching Brianna how to walk. The succession of images was relentless, and all of it played out to the same piece of music. The haunting simple tune from earlier that morning, the one the old lady had written.

Sarah's song.

CHAPTER FOUR

Now that the twelve days were underway, Sarah found the transition from present to past an easy one. The words *High Hopes* were scrawled across the ornament in the second envelope, and when Sarah was certain the young caregiver wasn't coming, she allowed the memory to move ahead.

She arrived in Nashville that cold January evening with more high hopes than money, but that didn't matter. Her expectations would be met; she was sure of it. She would take her songs to the first music company she could find, sing a few of her favorites, and let the executives explain the steps to getting a contract.

Money wouldn't have to be much up front. Just enough to make a living, nothing more. But touring was important. Anyone in the industry knew touring was the way to find a following and get a song on the charts. The recording company would have to send her on a tour; she would insist.

Sarah took a hotel that first night and reviewed her plan. She had enough money to last a month or so, but it wouldn't take that long. Two weeks and she'd be on her way, connected with a label and moving forward with her singing career.

Her mother and father had prayed for her before she left. That first night, alone in a dark hotel room in a strange new city, the words to her parents' prayer came rushing back.

You know Sarah's heart, God, and the future You have for her. Keep her safe and let her find the place, the purpose, and the plans You've laid out for her.

Sarah repeated the prayer several times, adding her own requests. As she did, a thought came to her. This was the first time she'd gone to sleep without her parents nearby, and yet she felt at home, comfortable. Unafraid.

Not once that first night did Sam Lindeman even cross her mind.

When morning came she set out to find her record deal, but by dusk she'd found just one thing. A reality check. Getting a label to back her might be harder than she'd thought.

The first week blurred into the second. She visited agents and production houses and the executive offices of recording studios. Once in a while someone would look her up and down and raise a curious eyebrow. Then they'd pass her off to a talent scout or an agent or someone on the other side of town.

"Come back when you get a demo, kid," they'd tell her.

By the end of the first month, Sarah's high hopes had dwindled to one: survival. She moved her things to a seedy hotel in what was obviously the worst part of town. Talking to God didn't seem to help, so Sarah stopped praying. It was one more break with the routine of her past, and it felt good, more independent.

Whatever happened next would be her doing—good or bad.

Not the result of God.

Sarah was sure her parents would be shocked with her new attitude, so she didn't tell them.

"You're praying, right, Sarah?" her mother would ask.

"Of course, Mama," she lied. "All the time."

"Us, too. God will show you the way, honey. Just keep looking."

"I will, Mama."

Her father's question was the same each time. "Finding any work?"

"Still looking, Daddy, but don't worry. Any day now."

Sarah spoke with her parents once or twice a week, and always the phone calls ended the same. Yes, she had enough money; yes, she was fine; yes, her big break was just around the corner.

Never did they mention Sam, and Sarah didn't ask. She didn't want to know. She'd walked away from Sam and the church-girl life that had all but smothered her. She was a new person, and though she wasn't always honest with her parents, she truly believed what she said about her future.

Her break into the music industry was coming. Any day and she'd be on her way.

Six weeks after arriving in Nashville, Sarah had been to every industry location in Nashville twice. She would take a cab to the general area and canvass every address in a ten-block radius. The answer was always the same—she needed experience.

By then she had reduced her expenses to one meal a day—a buffet three blocks from her hotel. The food was bland and greasy and one dish tasted suspiciously like another, but she could eat as much as she wanted, and the meal kept her going. Late that week, she spread what was left of her money across her hotel bed and realized how dire her situation had become.

She was down to eleven dollars.

If she didn't find work the next morning, she would have to leave the hotel, and then what? Call her parents and tell them she'd failed? Ask for money and risk having them see her dreams as sheer foolery?

Sarah gritted her teeth and stared at her file of songs perched on top of the cheap dresser. No, she wouldn't let that happen; she wouldn't fail. The dirty walls of her lousy room closed in a little more each day, but they would have to crush her before she'd give up. She'd get a job tomorrow and she'd do it without anyone's help.

That night before she fell asleep she stared at the mirror. Her long blonde hair and church dresses made her look sixteen, not twenty-three. Maybe the industry officials would take her seriously if she changed her look. Tucked in her bag of personal items was a pair of scissors and a small sewing kit.

With a building excitement, she grabbed them both, returned to the mirror and began cutting. Fifteen minutes later she'd given herself an entirely new look. Her short bob wasn't the most professional she'd seen, but it took care of the girl-next-door look. Next she grabbed her most colorful church dress, laid it out on the bathroom counter and began cutting the skirt. When she was done, she hemmed it, slipped it on, and grinned. The dress had once fallen almost to her ankles, loose and modest around her hips and waist. Now it came to just above her knees. With the extra material, Sarah quickly fashioned a belt, fastened it around her waist, and undid the top buttons on the dress. She studied the mirror once more.

This time she made a slight gasp, her eyes wide. She looked like a different person. Her figure was stunning, something even she hadn't realized. And with her new haircut she could hardly wait for morning.

The next day she walked into Trailway Records, the first office she'd been to when she arrived nearly two months earlier. A young man was working the phones and when she came through the door and removed her coat, he did a double take and spilled his coffee. He smiled at her and held up a single finger, silently asking her to stay.

Sarah nodded and took a nearby chair. She held her portfolio of songs close to her chest and crossed her legs the way she'd seen showgirls cross them in the movies. Making sure the young man had a clear view of her curvy calves.

In two minutes he was off the phone and on his feet. "Hi." He walked around his desk and smiled. "Can I help you?"

"Yes." Sarah stood and gave him a look she'd been working on all morning. "I'm a singer." She flashed him a slow smile. "I need a job."

48

"I see." The man was nodding before she had the words out. "I think we can help you." He introduced himself as Mr. Hamilton, and in a hurry he called to a man in a nearby office. Before Sarah could grasp what was happening, she was standing on a small stage in front of four men. One of them was at the piano, the music to her songs spread out before him.

"Okay, Sarah," one of the men said. "Let's hear what you've got."

She sang three pieces, but after the first they no longer seemed to be listening. The three men brought their heads together and whispered. Sarah felt a thrill work its way through her body. They were talking over the details of her contract. Once in a while one of them waved at her to keep singing. Sarah was so happy she could barely remember the words.

When they were finished talking, Mr. Hamilton approached her and motioned for her to stop.

"So . . ." She was breathless. This was it, the moment she'd been waiting for. They would present her with a contract and she'd be on her way. "Am I in?"

"Well," Mr. Hamilton smiled big. "Our office girl left yesterday." His tone suggested this was the best possible news. "We'd like to bring you in, train you on the phones, the filing, that sort of thing."

Blood rushed to Sarah's face and she felt faint. "Phones?" She blinked hard. "What about . . . what about my songs? My contract?"

"Uh . . ." Mr. Hamilton hesitated, then turned and looked at the three men waiting at the back of the room. When he met Sarah's eyes again his smile faded some. "We might be able to get you some studio work, singing backgrounds, demos, that sort of thing." A nervous laugh slipped. "Yeah, the uh . . . the contract, why, that comes later on. Down the road."

He explained the pay. Fifty dollars a week plus bonus money if they needed her for studio work.

Sarah wanted to spit at the man. How dare he give her a job answering phones and filing paperwork? But she stopped herself. This was the first job she'd been offered, and the manager at the hotel wanted his money. He'd made her a deal—a hundred dollars a month if she cleaned her own room. The job would leave her enough spending money to eat and eventually buy a new dress or two.

She thought about the alternative—calling home and asking for train money.

"Fine." She lifted her chin, too proud to smile. "When do I start?"

The men looked at each other again and Mr. Hamilton cleared his throat. "Right now if you're ready."

Sarah was, and by the end of the day she had the office system memorized. Before she left for the evening, Mr. Hamilton approached her. The others were already gone, and something more suggestive shone in the man's eyes.

"Want a ride?" He reached out and brushed his finger against her chin. "Maybe we could, you know, talk about that studio work you're wanting."

A chill passed over Sarah. She slipped her coat on

and shook her head. "I'll take a cab, thank you. And it's not studio work I'm wanting, Mr. Hamilton." She snatched her packet of songs from the desk and glared at him. "It's a contract."

That night she checked the mirror again and admired her new look. If she had to answer a thousand phone calls on the way up, at least she had a job in Nashville. A job she'd gotten on her very own, without handouts or connections or any praying on her part. It was hers, fair and square, and despite the circumstances Sarah was bursting at the seams.

She had come to Nashville seeking a career in the music industry, and now she was on her way.

"It's just like I dreamed, Mama," Sarah didn't mention the phone work or filing when she reported home that night. "I'll be singing in Nashville."

"Baby, be careful." Her mother's tone was always reserved, anxious about the entire situation. "I'm still praying."

Her father was more upbeat. "You let us know when you'll be onstage, now. We'll come and see you sing, all right?"

"It should be sometime soon, Daddy. I'll let you know." Sarah bit her lip. The lie felt bitter on her tongue, but then, it wasn't a total lie. She would be on a stage singing sometime soon. The people at Trailway Records were bound to see the light, and then the offers would come. A contract, a tour, a traveling band. All of it would happen, especially now that she was in with a studio.

The weeks blended into months and Sarah found

51

herself fielding more passes from Mr. Hamilton than phone calls or files. But every now and then he made good on his word and allowed her some studio work. Backgrounds for a small piece, or harmony on a demo tape.

Each time she stood before the microphone Sarah felt the same way. One step closer to her dream. All she needed was a break, one single break. And at the end of her third month with Trailway Records, Sarah found it.

CHAPTER FIVE

THE SECOND DAY of Sarah's Christmas ritual blended into the third, and the ornament read *Excitement*. Even now that was the only word that could've described the feeling Sarah had the day Mitch Mullins walked into Trailway Studios.

Mitch was a country music star, an overnight phenomenon, a man on his way to becoming an icon. He'd broken onto the scene two years earlier and already he had six number one songs. His dark looks and smooth voice made him a heartthrob, and for a nation looking for purpose, Mitch's soulful lyrics kept the industry hungry for more.

Sarah was aware of him. She loved his music, and she'd heard enough chatter working at Trailway Records to know his wild reputation. Mitch was the kind of man her parents had warned her against. Not that it mattered. Nashville was a big town and Sarah never expected to meet him.

But that month he was between contracts, looking for a new label when he came into the office for a meeting with the higher-ups. Electricity filled the air when Mitch and his agent arrived, though Sarah didn't talk with him. She was in the studio all day working on a demo.

Halfway through the day Sarah was trying to bring life to a worn-out song when Mitch walked through the studio doors, spotted her, and froze. Sarah's breath caught in her throat. He was even more striking in person. She felt her face flush under his gaze, but she kept her attention on the producer and his directions for the song.

When the music ended, a break was called and Mitch meandered his way toward her.

"Hello." An easy grin tugged at his mouth. His eyes made a lazy trip down the length of her and back up again. He was only a few feet away now and he held out his hand. "My name's Mitch."

"Hi." Sarah took hold of his fingers and the sensation sliced its way through her. She swallowed, searching for her voice. "I'm Sarah."

"Well, Sarah . . ." Mitch released her hand and took another step closer. A presence surrounded him, something powerful, stronger than anything Sarah had felt. "Since when does Trailway Records hire angels?"

She smiled and her cheeks grew hot again. This was Mitch Mullins talking to her, complimenting her. For a moment she broke eye contact and looked at the ground, not sure what to say. She reminded herself not to take the moment too seriously. If the stories about Mitch were true, he probably reacted this way to most women.

"I was in the office talking with the guys when I heard you." His tone was softer, genuine. "I had to see where that voice came from." He took her hand again and guided her along the edge of the stage and down three steps. "You're absolutely stunning, Sarah. Everything about you."

"Thank you." Sarah hoped her palms weren't

sweaty. *Calm down,* she told herself. *He says the same thing to all the girls.* She scanned the back of the studio for the director. The break wouldn't last much longer, even if she was talking to Mitch Mullins.

"Sarah, look at me."

Her eyes found his again. "Yes?"

"Let me take you away from here." He caught her other hand and eased his thumbs over the tops of her knuckles. "Sing backup for me on my tour, and when we get back to Nashville I'll make you the biggest star this town's ever seen."

The floor felt suddenly liquid; Sarah had to brace her knees to keep from falling. Mitch Mullins wanted her to sing backup for him, tour with him? He wanted her to make it big, and he'd only known her for five minutes? "I . . . I don't know what to say."

Mitch chuckled and squeezed her fingers. Then, as if it was the most natural thing in all the world, he leaned in and kissed her cheek. "Say yes, Sarah. You'll never regret it for a minute."

That evening Mitch had a driver bring Sarah to his Nashville estate, where his staff served them steamed fish and wild rice. They drank sweet tea from crystal goblets and Sarah tried to convince herself she wasn't dreaming. When they finished eating, he explained the situation. His backup singer had quit the week before to be with her family. His tour would start the following Monday—a ten-week bus trip through the south.

"Hamilton tells me you write your own songs." Mitch had dropped the slick one-liners from earlier that afternoon. Outside the studio atmosphere, he didn't seem like the country's fastest-rising star. He was genuine and likeable, a man oozing charm and utter confidence.

"Yes." She made a face and took a sip of tea. "I'm surprised he remembers."

"He said they were good."

Sarah's heart skipped a beat. "Really?"

"Yes." Mitch tossed his napkin on his plate and slid back from the table. He was across from her and his gaze never wavered. "I'm serious about the offer, Sarah. Sing for me on the tour and we'll get those songs on the air before summertime."

He stood and made his way around the table. With a familiar ease, he reached for her hand, waited until she was on her feet, then directed her into a sitting room. Before they reached the sofa, he stopped and turned to her. "Sarah," he gave a gentle pull and she was inches from him before she knew what had happened. "You're beautiful."

For a single instant, Sarah remembered Sam telling her that. She refused the thought. Mitch was so close she could feel his breath, smell the hint of his intoxicating cologne. "Thank you, Mitch."

Without waiting another moment, he drew her into his arms and kissed her, and suddenly there was no turning back. She quit her job the next day and gave herself to Mitch Mullins, heart and mind, body and soul.

"I've made it; I got my break," she told her parents. "I'm touring with Mitch Mullins."

Her father had doubts from the beginning. "He has a wild reputation, Sarah."

"Dad." She'd practiced her response, perfected the lie. "He likes my voice; nothing more."

From the time she hit the road with Mitch, warnings screamed at her. Girls were crazy for him, throwing themselves at the stage and bursting into tears if he reached out and touched their fingertips. At each show, dozens of girls would toss him gifts—flowers or teddy bears or slips of paper bearing phone numbers and unmentionable promises. Sarah figured since she and Mitch were an item, he'd toss the numbers as soon as the show was over. Instead she walked into his dressing room one night and caught him with a phone in one hand, a slip of paper in the other. When she asked him about it, he shrugged. "A man's gotta have friends, baby."

But Mitch's escapades were beyond shady, even if Sarah didn't want to ask questions. Mitch would disappear after a show and return by cab the next morning just as the bus was ready to pull out. Other times he'd leave with a group of girls after a show, stay out until three or four in the morning, and still have the nerve to show up at her hotel door—shirt unbuttoned, lipstick on his cheek—looking for her affection.

Sarah wanted to be mad at him, but she couldn't. No matter how many girls he toyed with, she was the one he kept coming back to, the one he was in love with. Besides, what more could she ask for? She was singing backup for Mitch Mullins, performing for a packed house night after night, the way she'd always dreamed. Mitch was going to make her into a star, even though he hadn't talked much about it since they'd gone on tour.

"Mitch," she told him every few shows, "I haven't played my songs for you yet. Don't you want to hear them?"

"Yeah, sure, baby." He'd lean in and kiss her long enough to take her breath away. "Maybe at the next stop, okay?"

But at the next stop he'd say the same thing. *Next time, baby . . . we'll look at your songs next time.*

The routine was identical in nearly every city. After the shows, Mitch would spend the night with her. And in those moments she could barely remember what city she was in, let alone her parents' warning or the girl she used to be. Every now and then she thought about her forgotten faith and the promises she'd made as a young girl—promises to stay pure and set apart, to wait for her wedding day. But the longer she stayed on the road with Mitch Mullins the more distant that girl and those promises became.

A shudder passed over Sarah and gradually she pulled herself from the memory. The early days were the hardest to relive, but they were part of the story, part of the ritual all the same. Not because Sarah missed those days, but because without them there would've been no story at all.

That night she lay down on the pillow and struggled to get comfortable. Her breathing was shallow and stubborn, more so than before, and her tired heart beat slower than usual. When sleep finally found her, it wasn't with dreams of Mitch Mullins and the three ornaments already on the tree. It was with silent prayers and bits of her song, and a single thought she couldn't quite shake.

If God was going to let someone be changed by her story, her song, then where was her caregiver, Beth? The young woman had to be the right one, so why hadn't she come to hear the story?

The more Sarah thought about Beth, the more she became certain of something. Three days earlier, she had seen a look in Beth's eyes, something she couldn't quite identify. But now, now Sarah knew where she'd seen the look before, and that could only mean one thing. Beth was in trouble. Maybe with a child or a parent. Maybe with a spouse, but she was in trouble.

Because the look in her eyes was a rebellious defiance—the same type of look Sarah herself had carried back in 1941.

CHAPTER SIX

BOBBY BALDWIN couldn't sleep.

Beth was on the sofa, probably snoring under a mound of blankets the way she'd slept most nights since her announcement. At first Bobby hadn't minded. He was mad at Beth, frustrated with her. How dare she make a decision that would so swiftly and totally end their family?

But that night Bobby felt sick to his stomach and his heart ached. Now that he'd had time to think about the situation, he knew the score. Beth was serious. She was going to leave him after Christmas and nothing was going to stop her. Because of that, lately he walked around in a state of shock and desperation—frantic to find a way to turn back the clock.

He might be upset with Beth; he might not like her demands or the way she made him feel inadequate as a husband. But he loved her; with all his heart he loved her. He couldn't imagine living without her and Brianna—not for a week, let alone a few months or a year. Maybe forever.

The prospect of giving up his family was more than he could take, worse than he'd ever imagined. Even now—late at night with an early work shift in a few hours—the idea of losing them sat on his chest like a cement truck.

Beth was going to take his Brianna away and he could do nothing to change her mind. Sweet Brianna, who adored climbing into bed between the two of them. Brianna, who clamored about in the kitchen every Saturday while he made her Mickey Mouse pancakes. Brianna with her Eskimo kisses and *Hold-me-forever-Daddy* hugs.

How would he survive without her? Without either of them?

Brianna would be asleep now, dreaming about Christmas, sprawled out beneath her fairy princess bedspread. He slipped his feet out from under the covers, grabbed a crumpled sweatshirt from the floor, and threw it on. The house was chilly, more so than usual. He shivered once and snuck out the bedroom door. Without stopping, he passed a sleeping Beth and tiptoed into Brianna's room.

For a moment he stood there, silent, barely breathing. The moonlight splashed through her window and across her face. She was so pretty, such a delight.

"Hi, Brianna." He walked to her bed, his voice softer than a whisper. He eased himself onto the edge of her mattress and stared at her. "Daddy loves you, honey."

Sitting there, looking at his only child, Bobby felt a lump rise in his throat. How many days like this did he have left? Times when Brianna would be sleeping under his roof? Life was bound to play out predictably from here, wasn't it? Divorce had a sameness about it, a brokenness that repeated itself no matter how many people chose it.

Beth would leave and at first he'd see Brianna

often—several times a week at least. But life would get busy, and eventually Beth would grow tired of Spartanburg the way single people tire of small towns. She would move away, maybe back to Atlanta where her sisters lived, and then what?

Bobby closed his eyes and remembered something he hadn't thought of in years.

He'd been traveling late one August, going to California to visit his mother before she died. Beth and Brianna had stayed home, since the visit would take place at a hospital and Brianna had only been a baby at the time.

His layover was in St. Louis, and once the gate attendant started the boarding call, Bobby noticed a man and a little boy fifteen feet away. The man was standing, and the child—maybe seven years old—was holding onto his legs, clinging to him as though he never wanted to let go.

That's when Bobby noticed the woman.

Sitting a few feet back, her expression hard, was a woman whose arms were crossed. The man dropped to one knee and spoke to the little boy, but the woman checked her watch and shifted her position.

Finally a gate attendant approached them, and the man stood. He nodded as the attendant relayed something Bobby couldn't make out. Then the man pulled the boy into one final hug, held on for several seconds, and bid him good-bye. The boy straightened himself and that's when Bobby got a clear view of him.

The child was crying, sobbing. His next words were

loud enough for Bobby to hear. "I don't want to go, Dad."

The man hugged the boy once more, a desperate sort of hug. The two exchanged words and nods and one last embrace. Then the man stepped away and the boy—trying to be stoic—went with the gate attendant toward the jetway. Every few steps he craned his neck around and gave the man a little wave, and the man—his expression strong—made an attempt to smile back.

Not until the boy turned the corner and disappeared did the man break. He turned around, took a few slow steps past the woman, and hung his head against the wall. For a long while—through most of the boarding call—the man stayed there, his shoulders shaking as he cried for the boy.

Bobby watched the entire scene, watched how the woman left the man alone, how she looked pained for him, but indignant. She shared none of the man's brokenness. What, Bobby wondered, would have explained such a scene? A man saying good-bye to his son? A woman sitting nearby disinterested?

And then it hit him.

The situation was obvious; it was the end of summer, after all. The boy's parents obviously lived in separate cities—possibly separate states. After a summer with his father, the boy must have been returning home—wherever home was—to be with his mother.

The disinterested woman was probably the new wife.

All of it made sense. And for weeks the image stayed with him—the broken man leaning on an airport wall, weeping, his head buried in the crook of his arm.

A portrait of divorce.

It was the same picture any time children were involved. Oh, sure, at first divorce promised freedom, an answer to every trouble marriage had a way of bringing. But divorce was a lie, a con-artist that moved into a family and stole the little moments, robbing every member blind. It was a hand grenade that shattered lives and destroyed dreams, taking no prisoners along the way.

At least that's the way Bobby remembered thinking about it at the time.

He never shared the image with Beth, never felt the need to share it. They were happy, right? Why talk about divorce? They'd promised each other forever, and forever was what Bobby expected. They went to church and prayed with Brianna before bedtime. And if their schedules and budgets didn't allow time for date nights or yellow roses, well then, at least they had Sunday mornings together.

Nothing had changed there, but over time Bobby forgot about the scene at the airport and divorce began to seem somehow more understandable. Not for him and Beth, maybe, but for some of the guys on the maintenance crew at work, guys with issues in their marriages. Not serious issues of abuse or unfaithfulness, but bickering and boredom and a spouse hardly worth going home to.

For them divorce meant the chance for new love, someone more exciting, more sympathetic. For years, despite everything he knew to be true, that's the way Bobby had viewed it.

Until now.

The nausea within him grew worse and he gave a hard shake of his head. Was Beth crazy? Couldn't she look ahead and see where leaving would get them? It was her fault, after all. She wanted to leave.

He studied Brianna, her little-girl lips and the soft way her chest rose and fell with each breath. It didn't matter if it was Beth's fault. Either way, a divorce would touch them all, change them from what they'd been to another statistic.

If Beth left with Brianna, one day he'd be the man in the airport, telling his daughter good-bye at summer's end, waiting until the following Christmas or maybe an entire year before seeing her again. Only he wouldn't fall against the airport wall in tears, he'd collapse right there at the jetway. Unable to breathe or move or exist with his daughter leaving him.

The ache in his heart grew stronger and Bobby hunched forward, one hand on Brianna's pillow.

How had they let it fall apart? He and Beth had been perfect for each other, hadn't they? In love and excited about a lifetime together? Wasn't that them? So what had gone wrong? Had Beth found someone else, someone with a better job, more money, and security?

Bobby exhaled and the sound of it rattled his soul. Whatever the reason, this whole mess was her fault. He hadn't done anything but put in his forty hours a week and show up each night at home. He didn't drink or gamble or hang out with the guys. He'd never once been interested in another woman, so what was her problem?

"God . . . what happened?" His words were barely audible. "Why isn't this enough for Beth?"

He heard nothing in response, no booming voice telling him how he might change Beth's mind. But a strong sense came over him, a sense that made him long for a look at their wedding pictures, the place where their lives had come together. He kissed Brianna on the cheek, and crept out the door, down the hall to the TV room.

Quietly, so he wouldn't wake Beth, he scanned the top bookshelf until he saw the brown leather-like cover. Their wedding album. He reached for the book and pulled it out. A layer of dust came down with it. He carried the album to their bedroom, sat at the end of the bed, and stared at the cover.

In golden letters the front read, "Robert and Elizabeth, forever." Their wedding date was centered beneath.

What was it they'd promised that summer, when the photographer presented them with the book? That they'd look at the pictures every year on their anniversary, wasn't that it? That they'd take an evening and remember the events and people who brought them together, so that their love would never have a chance to fade, right?

But two years later, Brianna came along and somehow the promise was forgotten.

Bobby ran his fingers over the dusty cover and figured it had been four years since either of them had even thought of the wedding pictures, let alone taken the time to look at it.

Still, he wasn't sure why he suddenly wanted to see them now, in the middle of the night. If Beth wasn't interested in staying, a bunch of photographs wouldn't do them much good.

He opened the first page and for a moment he couldn't breathe.

Beth looked beautiful. She was facing him, the two of them looking like the definition of love. She was beyond beautiful, and not just her face and hair and the dress she wore. But her expression, caught in his embrace, unaware of the camera. Hunger and longing filled their eyes, and a passion that went beyond physical desire.

But even that wasn't what made him struggle for the next breath. Instead it was the words scrawled at the bottom of the page, a Bible verse he'd used in his vows.

"Husbands, love your wives, just as Christ loved the church and gave himself up for her."

Since Beth's announcement that she was leaving, Bobby had insisted the trouble was her fault. Her fault for being unhappy, her fault for being self-centered, her fault for even thinking of taking Brianna away from him.

But here, now, those excuses were leaking from his airtight understanding like air from an untied balloon.

Sure, he went to work each day and came home every night. His job had kept them fed and clothed, but what had he done to keep their marriage alive? Slowly, he shut the book, too sad and tired to turn another page.

The book tucked up against his chest, he fell asleep, and for the first time that week it wasn't with condemning thoughts of Beth and her selfishness.

Rather, it was of his own.

He'd been wrong to let their marriage die. Tomorrow morning he would stop pointing fingers at Beth and start finding ways to love her, the way he'd long since stopped loving her. He had no idea how—in a few weeks' time—he could find a way to make things right again, but he had to try.

Most of all, he had to find a way to lay down his life for the only girl he'd ever loved.

Beth's first thought the next morning was that she must have been dreaming. She'd dreamed that Bobby had been creeping around the TV room while she was sleeping, and that he'd taken their wedding album down from the top shelf. It wasn't until she was fully awake that she realized she hadn't been dreaming at all. Where the book had been was now only an empty space.

She sat up and squinted, puzzled. What would he want with their wedding album, and why now? No answer came, and she turned her head one way and then the other, trying to stretch out the kinks in her neck. The Christmas season was proving to be unbearable. She was anxious and frustrated and sick of sleeping on the sofa.

She and Bobby had barely spoken to each other, and Brianna was getting suspicious. Later that morning, as she was eating Corn Flakes, she dropped her spoon into the bowl and turned to Beth.

"How come you don't like Daddy anymore?"

Beth set down her coffee and stared at Brianna. What had Bobby said? Something to poison their daughter's mind about who the bad parent was? Something to soften the blow in the battle that was about to be their lives? She leaned in, already angry. "Did Daddy tell you that?"

"No." Brianna gave an angry pout. "You keep sleeping in the TV room without Daddy and that means you don't like him."

Guilt hit Beth hard. Brianna was waiting for an answer, but Beth had none to give. How had Brianna found out about the sofa, and when had she grown so perceptive? "Well, honey . . ." She tapped her fingers on the table and tried to smile. "That's because Mommy isn't feeling good. It's almost Christmas and I don't want poor Daddy to get sick."

The excuse sounded ridiculous even to Beth. Brianna only rolled her eyes. "If you liked him you'd sleep in your own room, Mommy. You sleep with me when I'm sick, remember?"

They ate the rest of their breakfast in silence, and nothing felt quite right between them even after Beth dropped her off at day care.

Beth leaned hard into the seat of her car as she

headed for work. Suddenly she remembered the old woman at the retirement home. Sarah Lindeman, the woman with the beautiful voice and that melody, the one Beth hadn't been able to get out of her head. Great. She gritted her teeth as she parked her car in the back lot of Greer Retirement Village. How many more people would she let down before Christmas?

Beth locked her door and headed across the parking lot. What had the woman said? If Beth listened to the story, then she'd tell her the secret of love? Yes, that was it. The secret of love.

Fine. Today she'd go see the old woman. Her own life might be falling apart, but that didn't mean she had the right to ignore a sweet old dear like Sarah Lindeman. The woman was probably suffering from dementia, among other ailments, but that didn't matter. She had something important to say and the woman didn't get many visitors. Beth might be the only person who would listen.

Crazy or not, the old woman deserved at least that much.

That morning she made sure Sarah was on her list of residents, and after she helped the old woman finish breakfast and wash up, Beth took a spot at the end of the bed. She looked intently at her. "You think I've forgotten."

Sarah angled her head, unblinking. "Yes. I guess so." She shifted her attention to the crooked plastic Christmas tree perched on her bedside table. "Today's the sixth day."

"I know." Beth folded her hands on her lap. "I'm

sorry. Things . . . well, things haven't been good at home." She hesitated. "Is it too late, Sarah? Could you catch me up so I could hear the story?"

"Yes." Sarah sat a little straighter in her bed. Her smile said she wasn't mad about Beth's absence these past few days. "Yes, that would be very nice."

Beth stood, closed the door, and pulled a chair up to the bed. "What have I missed, Sarah?"

The old woman looked at Beth again and cleared her throat. Then she began. She talked about her love for Sam Lindeman, but her greater love for a career in Nashville. She shared about her decision to leave Sam and Greer and everything familiar in order to follow her dream of finding a recording contract. Then she shared about her job at Trailway Records and meeting Mitch Mullins.

"Mitch Mullins?" Beth narrowed her eyes. "I've heard of him."

"Yes." Sarah's expression changed, and something sad haunted her eyes. "He was quite well known in his day. By the fans . . . and the women." She paused and looked out the window. When she spoke again, she was a million miles away. "I toured with him. He was going to make me famous." A sad laugh died on her lips. "I thought . . . I thought he loved me."

Beth waited, studying the woman spread out on the hospital bed before her. For the first time, she tried to picture her not as the old woman in Room 11, but as she was back in her day. No doubt a beautiful girl with a voice and a figure that stopped even celebrities in their tracks.

When Sarah didn't speak, Beth leaned forward. "Sarah?"

"Yes?" She cast a sideways glance at Beth.

"What happened? Did you and Mitch stay together?"

Sarah made a sad, tired sort of sound. "No, dear. That's the story behind the fourth and fifth ornaments." She pointed a bony finger at the little tree. "Four is *Rebellious* and five is *Exposed*." Her head moved up and down in a slow, trancelike manner. "Yes, indeed. I was rebellious. I knew what I was doing but I did it anyway."

She explained how the touring life grew crazier with each week. Always she would ask Mitch what was going on with the other girls, and he'd say the same thing. They needed his time, his attention. Hanging out with the fans was part of the act, part of making it big.

Was he sleeping with them, Sarah wanted to know. His answer was the same every time—definitely not. She was the only one he was interested in, the only one he cared about. And one day soon he would listen to her songs and make her a star. One day very soon. Meanwhile, he paid her less than she'd been making at Trailway Records, always with promise of raises and bonuses. Any day, he'd tell her, just a few stops down the road.

The extra money never came, but things definitely got wilder, Mitch's nights away more frequent. One night he sent one of his band members to her room when he was out with his groupies.

"It was past midnight and there was a knock at the door. I opened it, and there was Mitch's drummer. 'Mitch says you're up for a good time tonight, Sarah,' he told me. 'Whad'ya say?'"

Beth leaned closer, sucked in by the story. "No!"

"Yes." Sarah pursed her lips, as if talking about the memory left a terrible taste in her mouth.

"Wow." Beth tried not to look surprised. Sarah had said her story took place in 1941, a time when the American life was supposed to be wholesome and innocent. Beth had no idea such craziness went on so many decades back.

Sarah stared out the window again and finished the story.

When she realized Mitch's intentions, that she should offer them the same favors she'd been offering Mitch, she felt dirty and cheap and ugly.

"Like a rotting bag of leftovers," Sarah frowned. "Sitting too long on the curb."

Two nights later, Mitch took his own room instead of sharing hers. Suspicious, Sarah waited until the early hours of the morning, donned a bathrobe, and strode down the hall to his door. After ten minutes of incessant knocking, Mitch answered. He had a towel around his waist. Over his shoulder, in the hotel room, Sarah saw a young blonde in his bed, the sheet pulled up to her neck.

"The lie was out," Sarah turned her attention back to Beth. She pointed to the tree again. "See, there. The fifth ornament says *Exposed* because Mitch Mullins was never going to lie to me again."

Beth sat back in her chair, captured by the story. "So what happened?"

"What happened?" Sarah looked startled, as if the answer was obvious. "With Mitch, you mean?"

"Yes. Did you let him have it there in the hallway?" Beth willed her words to come more slowly. Sarah wasn't in a rush. If she'd planned twelve days to tell her story, the answers weren't bound to come in as many minutes.

Sarah said nothing in response. Instead she reached a shaky hand to the table by the bed and picked up an envelope with the number six on it. "That's today's story. The part that changed everything."

"Oh." Beth looked at the clock over Sarah's bed and winced. Her boss would never understand her spending so much time in one room. She started to stand, started to tell Sarah she'd have to catch up the next day. But something made her stay seated, riveted to her chair.

With slow, careful fingers, Sarah opened the envelope flap and pulled out the ornament. Like the others, it held just one word. A word Beth hadn't thought about for years, but one that obviously held special meaning for Sarah.

The word was *Dance.*

CHAPTER SEVEN

SARAH COULD FEEL HERSELF getting sicker, slipping away a little more each day. But her heart hadn't been so full in a long, long time.

Not even a visit from her children or grandchildren had brought her the purpose she felt sharing her story with Beth Baldwin. The woman had an edge, a sadness Sarah recognized. Something she'd said when she first arrived, about having trouble at home, explained some of it. But there was something else, something deeper.

And it still reminded Sarah of herself, the way she'd been the summer of 1941. Sarah wasn't sure how, but God was going to do something amazing for Beth Baldwin, something that could only happen as Beth listened to the story, as she heard the song.

It was Day Six, the day that represented the turning point, the moment when things changed for Sarah. With Beth sitting nearby listening, Sarah connected once more with a series of events that were over six decades old.

The epiphany took place the day after she found Mitch Mullins in a room with another girl. As shallow as his stories about groupies had been, Sarah had always believed him, always wanted to believe him. But after catching him in the act that night, she went back to her room and never fell asleep.

For the first time since leaving Greer, she missed Sam Lindeman, missed him with every fiber of her being. Strong, handsome, dependable Sam, a man who had loved her enough to let her follow her dreams. But now, after giving her virtue to a man who had cheated on her and lied to her from the beginning, Sarah was sure of something else.

Sam would never be interested in her.

She wasn't the same girl she'd been when she left home, and no matter how much she missed Sam, she wouldn't mess with his heart by calling him now. Instead she sat on her hotel bed and wept. What had she been thinking, taking up with a man like Mitch Mullins? So what if the whole world adored him; his nature had been obvious from the beginning.

Since when does Trailway Records hire angels?

Indeed. Mitch was master of the come-on lines; he'd had her following him around like a puppy dog after just one dinner.

Sarah paused and looked at Beth. "At that moment, the lights in my conscience came on again." She ran her tongue over her lower lip. "After weeks of living in darkness, I was suddenly able to see the horrifying mistakes I'd made—all of them spread out like a train wreck."

One by one her bad choices screamed at her that night. She'd turned her back on everything her parents had taught her, everything that had ever mattered to her. She had given up on God and His plans for her life, and her promise to remain pure until marriage was gone. Her virtue was forever lost.

But worst of all, she'd walked away from Sam.

Sarah stared at the tiny blue-bonnet wallpaper. The smell of the hotel's musty carpets filled her senses as she choked back quiet, desperate sobs. All of life was a dance, the steps measured out to the music of the days. But since she'd arrived in Nashville, she'd checked herself at the door and let an imposter take over.

Now, though . . . now it was her turn again. Time to find her way back to all she'd once been.

Mitch Mullins had no plans of making her into a star, no plans of hearing her songs or giving her a pay raise. He was using her, the way her parents had warned he would.

That night she packed her things, and the next morning, long before Mitch and his band members were awake, she took a cab to the train station and spent nearly all of her remaining money on a train back to Greer. Over the hours, the clickity-clack of the train became music, and her heart pounded out a rhythm she could live with, one she could dance to.

The next day, when she arrived home, she had one place to visit before taking a cab to her parents' house.

Greer Community Church.

"Wait for me, please." She gave the cab driver an extra quarter and ran lightly across the church lawn. It was Thursday, in the middle of the afternoon, but she was sure the doors to the sanctuary would be open. They were always open at Greer Community.

77

Once inside, she took slow steps toward the front and slid into the second row. She was the only one in the building, but she felt surrounded by love and peace and acceptance, the way she hadn't felt since meeting Mitch Mullins.

"God . . ." She closed her eyes. "I'm . . . I'm so sorry. I was wrong about everything. I walked away from You, from all I know to be good and true and right." A single tear slid down her cheek and she dabbed at it with the back of her hand. "But if You'll have me, I'm back, Jesus." She sniffed, and the sound of it echoed across the empty room. "I'm back for good. I promise."

Sarah exhaled, the sixth part of the story told.

She looked at the young woman sitting across from her and saw that she'd been right earlier. The story was touching something in Beth's soul, because the woman was crying. Not loud or with dramatics. But tears had formed two trails on both sides of her face and there was something broken in her expression.

Sarah reached her hand out to the woman and patted her arm. "Are you okay?"

"Yes." Beth snatched a tissue from the bedside table and wiped it beneath her nose. "That moment at the church . . . it sounds . . . it sounds very freeing."

Sarah smiled. "It was." She inhaled until her lungs were full. "It's time for me to move to the window."

"To the window?" Beth made a strange face. "You've been walking to the window by yourself?"

"Once in a while." She felt her smile creep a little

78

higher. "But today I could use your help, if you don't mind."

"Not at all." Beth tossed her tissue in a nearby trash can and stood, easing Sarah up until she was on her feet and positioned over her aluminum walker. "Why the window, Sarah?"

Sarah focused on the path in front of her and shook her head. When she reached the windowsill, she turned to Beth and held up a single finger. "That will come."

She stared out the window at the park until her eyes found the bench—the park bench that meant the world to her. And with all the energy she had left, she began to hum the melody, the notes that would always fill her heart and soul.

The notes to *Sarah's Song*.

Throughout the humming, Beth remained at her side, quiet, respectful. When she'd hummed the last line, Sarah pulled her eyes from the park bench and nodded at Beth. "That's all. I can go back now."

Beth helped her, and when Sarah was too tired to swing her legs up onto the bed, Beth lifted them. Once the old woman was settled back beneath the covers, Beth hesitated and then gave a slight shrug of her shoulders. "The music is beautiful, haunting." She glanced at the window and then back. "But why no words, Sarah? Didn't the song have words?"

"Indeed." Sarah yawned and squeezed Beth's hand. "I'm tired, dear. I think I'll take a nap."

Beth nodded, but she wouldn't let the idea go. "What about the words?"

"Later." Sarah could feel her eyes beginning to close. The familiar peace surrounded her again—a peace that defied all understanding. God was doing something here, something in young Beth's heart. And that was knowledge enough for Sarah.

She was almost asleep when Beth asked her question one final time. "When, Sarah . . . when will the words come?"

Slowly Sarah opened her eyes. "Day Nine."

There. She let her eyes close again. That would bring Beth back for sure. Not because she wouldn't survive without knowing the words to the song. But because God had placed a special truth deep inside Sarah's heart: A miracle was underway, a miracle for Beth Baldwin.

And God would bring her back if He had to move heaven and earth to do it.

CHAPTER EIGHT

IT WAS TUESDAY, December 21, and the good weather had finally given out.

That morning Beth woke to a six-inch blanket of snow spread across Spartanburg, and she mumbled under her breath as she headed for the shower. White Christmases were overrated. The city would take a week to dig out from beneath the snow, and until then the commute to Greer would be unbearable. Snow would turn to ice, leaving the roads slick and dangerous. Beth was scheduled to work every day that week, and the snow meant she'd have to get up an hour earlier each morning.

Her shower was quick, and as soon as she was dressed she hurried into Brianna's room. "Get up, sleepyhead. Time to eat."

Brianna moaned.

"Come on, honey. We gotta eat if we're going to be on time."

Brianna rolled over in her bed. "No! Don't wanna eat!"

"Mommy's not giving you a choice." Beth yanked the covers from her daughter and waited, arms crossed. "Get out of bed."

"Do I have to, Mommy?" Brianna's tone was more whine than words.

"Yes. One . . . two . . . three . . ."

Brianna spilled out of bed and stopped short of

scowling at Beth. "Help me get dressed."

Beth hesitated, then went to the closet and sorted through the clothes. Her daughter's accusations regarding Bobby had dropped off, but she was grumpy or pensive most of the time. Earlier that week, Bobby had asked about it. "Did you say something to Brianna—something about us separating?"

"No." Beth's answer was short, the way she felt most of the time toward her husband. "Did you?"

"Of course not." He scowled at her. "We agreed."

"Right."

"So why's she asking about us, telling me I don't like you all of a sudden?"

Beth shrugged. "She's telling me the same thing. Maybe she feels it."

"Feels it?"

"Yes. That her parents don't love each other anymore."

"Listen . . ." Anger flashed in Bobby's eyes as he pointed a finger at Beth. "I never said I didn't love you. Those were your words." Then, as if he somehow caught himself, his expression eased and his voice grew calmer. "I'm sorry. I didn't mean to yell. All I'm saying, Beth, is I still love you. For whatever that's worth."

The conversation had stayed with her because it seemed so unlike Bobby. Sure, he had tried initially to change her mind about leaving. But when things didn't go his way, he was usually quick on the defensive. That time, though, he had backed off, even told her he was sorry and he loved her. Not just once, but several times after their initial confrontation, he'd pulled her aside in an effort to talk to her or apologize. Beth tried not to look too deeply into it. Probably last-minute remorse over their failed marriage, or maybe the Christmas season getting to him.

Either way, their conversation had done nothing to ease Brianna's mood. The carefree child with bright eyes and bouncing pigtails had disappeared, and in her place was a little girl both moody and melancholy.

Beth kept the morning routine at a fast pace, and managed to get Brianna in the car eight minutes earlier than usual. Sure enough, the commute was stop and go, with an occasional car sliding off the road and others spinning into oncoming traffic. The speed was slow, so none of the mishaps was serious, and Beth pulled up in front of Brianna's day care just a few minutes later than usual.

Dana Goode—one of Beth's friends from high school—ran the day care from her house. Beth felt good leaving Brianna with her, and sometimes, if she was early, she and Dana would talk about the old days, high school and dating and how Bobby was always the only one for Beth.

"Everyone always said it," Dana would say as she punished a piece of gum, "Bobby Baldwin only had eyes for you, Beth. As far back as time he only had eyes for you."

Beth had still not told Dana about her decision to leave; she was sure the idea wouldn't go over well.

Just as well she had no time to talk that morning. She led Brianna up the walk, careful not to slip in the snow, and shouldered her way into the house. She was about to kiss Brianna good-bye when she looked up and saw Dana standing there, both eyebrows raised halfway up her forehead.

Beth went ahead with her kiss and patted Brianna's back. "Go on, honey, the kids are waiting for you."

Brianna looked from her mother to Dana and back again. "Bye." She shuffled off, a blank look on her face.

The moment she was out of earshot, Dana leaned in and hissed at Beth. "You and Bobby are splitting up? What, Beth, are you crazy?"

Beth refused to react. She put her hands on her hips and gave a slight roll of her eyes. "Who told you?"

"Who do you think?" She huffed hard and paced two steps away, then two steps back. "Bobby called, asked me to pray for you guys."

"He what?" Beth was amused at the idea. Bobby hadn't talked about prayer in years, other than an occasional dinner when he remembered to pray over the meal. They went to church once in a rare while, but that was the extent of it. "Now I know you're making it up. Come on, who told you? Really . . ."

Dana stopped, her mouth open. "I can't believe you, Beth. What's happened?" She straightened, the shock wearing off. "Wasn't that you driving me to church every Sunday during our college years? Weren't you the one telling me to trust God, that someone right would come along if I put God first?"

Beth's gaze fell. "That was a long time ago." She looked up. "For all of us."

"Meaning?"

"Meaning Bobby and I haven't prayed together in years. Don't tell me he asked you to pray for our marriage."

"Well." Another huff. "That's exactly what he did. Now listen, Beth. It's my job as a friend to tell you this." Dana was a fast talker; she paused only long enough to snatch another breath. "No one will ever love you the way Bobby loves you. He might've slipped lately, forgotten what was important, but that doesn't change the facts."

"Slipped?" Beth looked at her watch and gave a chuckle that sounded more sarcastic than humorous. "I haven't seen a yellow rose in three years, Dana. When Bobby and I were dating, he brought me yellow roses every week. Yellow roses and homemade key lime pie—the only thing he knew how to cook."

"So you grew up. So what?"

"So?" Beth tossed her hands up. "So now I'm old hat, and you know what?" She lowered her voice so Brianna wouldn't hear her in the next room. "I'm sick of it. Sick of coming home each afternoon to a husband parked in front of the television. Sick of competing with Sports Center for my husband's attention. If he had to choose between me and the TV remote, he'd take the remote. Hands down." She tossed her hair over her shoulder, fuming. "I'm sick of not mattering, Dana, sick of wishing he'd bring me roses or look at me the way he used to. I don't love him anymore. I don't." She straightened her sweater, grabbing at her composure. "I'm getting out before I forget how living feels."

A mix of emotions worked their way into Dana's expression. Shock became horror, and that became hurt and disappointment. Finally she shook her head. "Love's about more than yellow roses and key lime pie."

"Yeah." Beth took a few backward steps toward the door. "It's about more than the sports channel, too."

She was out the door and halfway to work before she realized how terrible she'd acted. Dana was only trying to help, trying to influence Beth not to leave.

But what about Bobby? What right did he have calling her friend and asking for prayer? He might as well have come right out and asked her to intervene.

Beth tightened her grip on the steering wheel.

It didn't matter; the ordeal would be over soon enough, as soon as Christmas was behind them. Bobby could say whatever he wanted, he could ask people to pray and tell her he still loved her. The truth was he wanted her to leave as badly as she wanted to go. Otherwise he would've spent more time with her, talked to her more often. Turned off the television once in a while.

No, it was over, and nothing would change the fact now.

She pulled into the parking lot of the Greer Retirement Village and headed to the third floor. That's when she remembered. It was Day Nine. She'd missed days seven and eight because they were her days off. But Day Nine was the big day, wasn't it? The day the sweet old woman would add words to her ritual?

86

For a moment she considered working the opposite side of the floor. The drawn-out story couldn't possibly help her, so why was she listening to it? Then it dawned on her: Because this was Christmas, and even if her entire life was falling apart, spending time with Sarah Lindeman was the least she could do—her way of giving something back to a lonely old lady.

She entered Sarah's room and found the woman sitting up, smiling at her. "You came."

"Yes." Beth stepped inside, not sure what she was feeling. "I want to hear the words to the song."

Last time she was here, listening to the story, the details had made her cry. But now—in light of the events that morning—she didn't feel a bit tenderhearted. She wanted to put in a mindless eight hours and move one day closer to December 26. For a beat, she considered turning around, but then she changed her mind. She returned Sarah's smile and set about finding fresh clothes for the woman. Over the next hour she prepared Sarah's bath and made sure she got her meal down.

When they were finished, Beth took her place in the familiar chair. "I've missed a few days."

"You weren't at work." Sarah shot her a thoughtful look. "Home with your family, no doubt."

"Yes." Beth couldn't force a smile. Enough about her family. She leaned forward in her seat. "Okay, catch me up."

"You have to promise something."

Promise something? Beth bit her lip. She barely knew the old woman. "What?"

"Promise you'll be here for the last three days."

Beth calculated the dates in her head. The twelfth day would take place on Friday, her last day of work before Christmas. She nodded at Sarah. "I promise." But the words felt hollow, even to her. She was about to walk away from her husband, after all. If she couldn't keep the most important promise she'd ever made, how could she expect to keep this one?

Still, Sarah seemed satisfied. She pulled herself up some and settled into a stack of pillows propped against the headboard. "You remember where we were?"

"The dance." Beth felt herself relax. Her time with Sarah did that to her. Now that she was back again, the story drew her, made her anxious for the next piece. And not only the next piece, but also for the special meaning Sarah had spoken about. Because in the midst of this crazy, hectic, hurtful Christmas season, between divorce plans and arguing with Bobby, Beth had an almost desperate need to understand the bigger picture.

It was possible Sarah knew what she was talking about, right? If she did, then in just a few days Beth might actually learn something she'd wanted to know for the past several years.

The secret of love.

CHAPTER NINE

SARAH TUCKED THE COVERS IN tight around her waist. Her heart glowed at the return of Beth Baldwin. The miracle was coming; Sarah could feel it.

"Yes, dear. That's where we were. The dance."

"You were at the church when we finished Day Six."

"Right. After stopping at the church I went straight home, to my parents' house." Sarah smiled, and her eyes grew watery. "My parents were great people; such love for God and me."

Sarah didn't comment on the irony, but it was there. In less than a week, Beth also was going back to her parents' house; Sarah had heard one of the nurses talking about it. She found her place in time.

"It was summer by then." Her eyes found the window, the place where she looked when her memories were the strongest. "Late July. The summer of forty-one."

Sarah's parents were at the doorstep the moment they saw her pull up. Without a single question, they took her in their arms and welcomed her inside. For the next hour—sparing them any of the shocking details—she told them how she had trusted Mitch Mullins, how he'd led her to believe he was interested in her music, and how he'd betrayed her in the end.

"I thought he loved me, Daddy." She lifted her eyes to her father, glad she hadn't told him how serious her mistakes had been. He was a kind, gentle man. The detailed truth would be more than he could handle.

"And now?" Sarah's mother was quiet, probably afraid of her answer. "How do you feel about him now?"

Sarah shook her head. "I never knew him. I made . . ." She hung her head. "I made a fool of myself."

"No, you didn't." Her father was on his feet, his arms outstretched. "You're here, aren't you? You had the sense to come home, to know that we were waiting for you." He gave her a hug. "Nothing foolish about that."

"Thanks, Daddy." Sarah held her breath. She'd been dying to ask the question since the night she found out about Mitch, but now the moment had come. "Have you heard from Sam?"

Her parents exchanged a look, and then her father sat back down in his chair, his elbows planted on his knees. "Sam left, sweetheart. Took a job somewhere up north. New York, maybe, or New Jersey."

Sarah's mouth went dry. What? Sam left? He took a job and didn't tell her parents whether it was in New York or New Jersey? Her head began to spin and she sat in the nearest chair, digging her fingernails into the palms of her hand in order to concentrate. "What . . . sort of job?"

"He's a principal, honey." Sarah's mother gave her a sad smile. "The last time we saw him, he said something about getting on with his life." She dropped her chin, her gaze gentle but unwavering. "I think he was referring to you, dear."

Sarah was drowning. As if she had a steel cable around her waist and no matter how hard she kicked and swam she couldn't get to the surface, couldn't grab another mouthful of air. "Where . . ." She gave a few short exhales and rubbed her fingers into her brow. "Where did he apply? Do you know?"

"To tell you the truth, honey, I don't think he wanted us to know. His parents moved away a few years ago—you know that. And when he came by the house his visit had a sense of finality to it." He looked at Sarah's mother. "Wouldn't you say so?"

"Yes." She bit her lower lip and gave a sad shake of her head. "I'm sorry, Sarah. I somehow guessed you'd come looking for him one day."

Sarah didn't have to finish the thought. The truth hung out there in the open for all three of them to gawk at. She'd waited too long for Sam Lindeman. He'd given years of his life to courting Sarah, and now he'd moved away, given up. The way he should've given up a long time ago.

In the next few days, Sarah tried everything to find him. She called the principal at his previous school, but the man was adamant. "We don't discuss former employees," he told her. "The files of our teachers—past and present—are highly confidential."

Sarah had another idea. She called the operator in the town where his parents had moved and asked for their number. After nearly a minute of checking, the operator came back on the line and apologized. "Apparently they've moved. There's no one in that town by the name Lindeman—listed or unlisted."

At the end of the week, she had to admit her situation. Sam was gone, and there wasn't a thing she could do about it.

Sarah broke her stare at the window, peered at Beth Baldwin, and nodded her chin toward the little Christmas tree. "That's why the seventh ornament says *Gone*." She kept her eyes on the tree. "And number eight, see it there?"

Beth slid to the edge of the padded chair and looked on the backside of the tree. "*Longing?* Is that the one?"

"It is." Sarah relaxed her neck and allowed herself a view of the window once more. She would've liked to tell the whole story perched along her walker, staring down at the bench. But this would have to do, this knowing that the bench was there, just outside the window.

She drew a full breath and continued.

When her efforts turned up nothing, she had to admit the truth. Sam was gone. With every hour that passed, Sarah longed for him, and became more certain that he had been exactly right for her, the man she'd always wanted. She'd left him to chase paper dreams and lost more than her high hopes along the way. Yes, Sam was gone, but she could no more stop longing for him than she could stop the sun from rising.

Not that Sarah expected much to come of her feelings.

Sam deserved someone whole and pure; he was too

good for a girl like her. She was yesterday's news, dead broke without a plan in the world, her singing career over almost as soon as it had started.

For the next month she held that opinion, certain that though God had forgiven her, it must've been a struggle for Him to do so. And Sam—if she ever saw him again—couldn't possibly see her the same as before. Not if he knew the truth.

"But something changed at the end of that month." Sarah's voice sounded distant, dreamy, even. "People kept seeing me and asking about Sam, and finally one Sunday I took the situation to God."

Beth's eyes were wide; she looked like she wouldn't have moved from her chair for anything in the world. "And?"

Sarah smiled, slow and full. "He gave me my song."

"And that's Number Nine?"

"Yes, dear." She pointed at the four envelopes remaining. "Could you hand me the one with the nine, Beth. Please?"

The envelopes looked ancient, cracked and faded. Beth took Number Nine and handed it to her. "I'm dying to know what happened."

"The most amazing thing, really." Sarah paused. "Sit back, Beth. You won't want to miss it. Not the story . . . or the part that comes afterwards. Remember, I told you?"

Beth grinned, and her eyes didn't look as pained as before. "The secret to love?"

"Exactly." Sarah pointed her finger in the air to

make her point. "The secret to love."

Sarah took the ornament from the envelope and said the word out loud. "The word is *Opportunity*." She placed it on the tree. "Let me explain."

The more time passed that summer, the more Sarah had longed for Sam. All she needed was a way to find him, to let him know she was thinking about him. An opportunity.

"And so I did the only thing I could think to do." She angled her head, her eyes on the window once more. "I wrote a song."

"The one you've been humming?"

"That very one."

Every day Sarah would walk to Greer Park and sit on the bench at the edge of the grassy field, allowing God to mold the words and lyrics to her song. That fall, sitting on the bench, she finally finished it. And then she begged God for a miracle, for His help in finding Sam. Even if only for a few minutes, so he could hear her song.

Another month went by. Then, one Monday morning in late September, Mr. Hamilton, her boss from Trailway Records, called. Someone had fallen for her voice. Not a Mitch Mullins. This time the person interested was the head of the company. The president of Trailway Records.

Sarah couldn't believe it, not even as she waited for Mr. Hamilton's explanation. While working in Nashville, she'd never met the president of the recording company, and now—now that she'd given up her dream and crawled home with her tail between her legs—now her voice had caught the attention of someone at the top of the industry.

"We'd like to bring you back out, Sarah." Mr. Hamilton's voice was brimming with excitement. "You can sing some of your other songs, and maybe something new. Would that be a problem?"

Sarah was thrilled, but not at the idea of living in Nashville. "I can come out, but I won't stay. My home is here in Greer."

"That's fine. We'll only need you for a week or so."

She thought of something. "I'm . . . I'm not sure I have the money to get there."

Mr. Hamilton gave a soft laugh. "Sarah, we'll pay for the train ticket, your meals, and your hotel. You'll be staying in the Trailway Records suite at the big hotel just down the street from our offices."

Sarah had to stifle a scream. She was getting her break after all! And without compromising anything! Her excitement was dimmed only by the fact that Sam would never know. He had prayed for her, wished her well, and let her go. But now he wouldn't be a part of whatever God was about to do. And she knew it was God, as surely as she knew what day it was. She'd given all of it—her life, her singing, her heart—back to God. And now, in all His mercy, He was giving her the chance to sing her own songs on her own terms, living at her own address.

She accepted the offer to come, and that afternoon she promised her parents that this time was different, legitimate. Among the musical pieces she slipped into her satchel before she left for Nashville was "Sarah's Song." She wasn't a bit surprised, when she sang for the president of Trailway Records later that week, that it was "Sarah's Song" he fell in love with.

Six weeks later it debuted in the number one spot on the country charts, and suddenly Sarah had the answer to her prayer. The opportunity she'd needed all along. The words she wanted to tell Sam were out there for all the country to hear. Absolutely everywhere.

Sarah stopped and looked at Beth. "It's time for the words. The first verse and the chorus."

Nothing more needed to be said.

Beth helped Sarah to the window, and there, for the first time since starting the simple ritual, Sarah opened her mouth and sang the words to her song—the one she'd written for Sam Lindeman back when she'd thought all hope of finding him was gone forever. Despite the years, her voice was sweet and clear, and the words were marked by feelings that had never dimmed.

It's not too late for faith to find us.
Not too late for right to win.
Not too late, let love remind us.
Not too late to try again.

The tune changed, and Sarah stared at the park bench, willing him to be there beside her one more time—one more day when they could sit together and marvel at the miracle of 1941.

She uttered a quick sigh; it was time for the first verse—the only one she wanted to sing that day. From the corner of her eyes, she glanced at Beth. The woman wasn't only listening, she was hanging on every word. Sarah kept singing, but she closed her eyes so nothing would interfere with the memory.

In my life the straight and narrow had a face, and it was yours.
I took crooked paths around you, shut you out, and locked the doors.
Long I wandered tired and aimless, seeking all the world might hold.
There you waited, true and blameless, soul of goodness, heart of gold.

They were both silent, and Beth swallowed hard. Sobs built within her, sobs she couldn't explain. What was it about the story that touched her so? And how come whenever Sarah spoke, the story seemed to be about Beth and Bobby instead? Not the details maybe, but the heartache behind them.

Or maybe it was the song. The words played again in Beth's mind. *It's not too late for faith to find us. Not too late for right to win. Not too late, let love remind us. Not too late to try again.*

Wasn't that what Bobby had been trying to tell her ever since her decision to leave?

Beth choked back the sobs and cleared her throat.

"I'm tired." Sarah made a backwards shuffling motion. "Help me, Beth, will you?"

When Sarah was in bed again, when she'd caught her breath, Beth searched the old woman's tired eyes. "Sam must've heard the song eventually. Right, Sarah?"

"Now, now." Sarah's eyelids lowered, as if she might fall asleep in the midst of her sentence. "You said you'd come tomorrow."

"I'll be here." Beth took her chair again.

"The answers are coming, Beth. I promise you."

"When, though? Which day?"

"Some will come tomorrow."

Beth didn't push beyond that. She refilled Sarah's water pitcher, tucked the blanket in around her again, and bid her good-bye. The story of Sarah and Sam couldn't be rushed, and maybe that was the richness of it.

Beautiful stories took longer to tell.

For a moment, as she hurried into the hall and off to the next resident's room, Beth let that thought simmer in her heart. If beautiful stories took longer, then why was she in such a rush to leave Bobby, to move Brianna away from her father and give up on their marriage?

The thought was fleeting, gone almost as soon as it came. The reasons were all too obvious. A story like theirs wouldn't get better over time; it would get worse. Unbearably worse, right?

But somehow, even with all the justifications she could muster, her decision to leave felt weak and wrought with poor excuses.

Several times over the next few hours Beth caught

herself remembering the early days with Bobby, the silly little somethings only the two of them understood, the rich rainy Sunday afternoons before Brianna was born, the quiet intimacy that had lasted long after they left the bedroom.

Why had they let time barge its way between them? And how could they rewind the clock now that they'd reached this point? She'd already made up her mind, hadn't she? Willing things to be better wouldn't make that happen between them. Beth mulled that over and wondered: What would it take to find their way back to a marriage marked by love and laughter?

By the time she drove home late that afternoon, one line of "Sarah's Song" had etched itself firmly in her mind. She had hummed it and sung it to herself a hundred times that day, and every time the first four words caught in her throat and made her feel like crying.

It's not too late . . .

They were words that screamed of hope and forgiveness and new life. But the sound of them on her own tongue made her heart heavy with sorrow because Beth was pretty sure about one thing.

Precious words like those would never apply to her.

CHAPTER TEN

Panic shot through Sarah, and she couldn't catch her breath.

She struggled to sit up, to wedge a pillow beneath her, but she couldn't do either. Instead, she sucked in with all her might. For her efforts, a single raspy bit of air toyed with her lungs, hardly enough to bring relief to her screaming body.

"Help me!" The words hung on the edge of her tongue, not loud enough for even Sarah to hear. She was dying; that had to be what was happening. Dying before she had a chance to finish her story, before she had the chance to tell Beth how everything had come together.

Before she'd gotten to the secret of love.

God, no! Don't let me die now. Not yet. She winced at the pain in her chest and made another desperate attempt at a breath. This one brought in less air than the last and she could feel herself waning away, feel her heart slowing within her.

Her eyes darted around the room, looking for an escape, a way to pull herself higher on the pillows. If only she could sit, she could catch her breath, and she chided herself for not taking the doctor's suggestion earlier that month.

"It would help if you'd sleep sitting up, Sarah. People at the end stages of heart failure find it much more comfortable."

"Doctor," Sarah had smiled at him. "I can't sleep sitting up. You know that."

She reached her hands over her head and wrapped her fingers around the top of the headboard. *Pull, Sarah. Come on, pull.* She strained until every muscle in her arms ached, but her efforts did nothing to lift her torso, nothing to relieve the pressure in her chest.

Just yesterday she could sit up on her own, so that meant something was wrong. Something that might send her home to heaven before lunchtime if she didn't find a way to get the staff's attention.

Suddenly she remembered the bell. Of course. Why hadn't she thought of it before? Her eyes darted to the wall beside her bed and there it was, bright red, screaming for her to notice it.

She started to lift her hand, but her body demanded another breath. Squinting, closing her eyes from the effort, Sarah sucked in everything she could, but still her body cried for more. Her eyes opened and she stared at the buzzer. Now! She had to press it now or it would be too late.

With all her remaining energy, she raised her hand up and jabbed her finger into the button. A buzzer sounded, and Sarah let her hand fall back to the bed, limp and trembling.

God, help me. I can't go home yet; that would ruin everything.

She concentrated on using as little air as possible, but just as she heard fast steps outside her door she felt herself slipping. Farther and farther away she fell, black spots dancing before her eyes, connecting, blocking out the faces of the people entering her room.

"Help . . ."

"Oh, dear! Someone get an ambulance," Sarah heard. But the sound was so faint she wasn't sure if she was dreaming. "We need oxygen in here, stat."

Don't let me sleep, God . . . don't take me home. Not yet. Not . . .

The thought faded from her consciousness and she was surrounded by a peaceful quiet and a darkness so heavy she couldn't think or move or even try to draw a breath.

Just when the darkness began to frighten her, a warm glow appeared, soft and gentle and drawing her near. Her soul was filled with a longing, a desire to go after the light as if this was the thing she'd been born to do, the thing she'd waited for all her life.

But something just as strong stopped her, made her turn and search the darkness for a way out. Sarah was no longer sure why, or what mattered so strongly on the other side. Only that she was desperate to go back. *God . . . please . . . please.*

And in that instant her eyes opened and she could see a host of people working on her. Beth Baldwin was standing in the back of the room, her fingers over her mouth. One of the men held something over Sarah's mouth and she realized she was sitting up. She could take a breath now, and the terrible weak feeling was going away. She pushed the soft plastic piece away from her mouth, her eyes wide. "What . . ." She gasped, filling her throat with sweet air. "What happened?"

"Ma'am, you need the oxygen mask." A paramedic slipped it back over her mouth, his eyes kind but firm. Once she was breathing steadily again, he leaned closer. "I'll explain this as simply as I can, ma'am. Your congestive heart failure is getting worse. Last night while you slept, your lungs began filling with fluid. You almost drowned."

Another medical technician stepped in beside him. "You'll need to stay propped up from now on."

From now on . . .

The words filtered through Sarah's mind and immediately she understood what was happening. This was the end her Doctor Cleary had told her about two years ago, when he first made the diagnosis of heart failure.

"Eventually, your lungs will fill up with fluid," the doctor had said. "We'll move you to a permanently upright position, but after that the end could come quickly."

Sarah hadn't been afraid. "How quickly?"

"Days." He gave her a sad sort of knowing look. "Sometimes only a few days."

Now here she was, three days left in her story, and the time had come. Dr. Cleary had explained it this way: Congestive heart failure was like lying down in a pool that was slowly filling with water. When the water began to cover a person's mouth and nose, the person with heart failure could sit up, but they wouldn't have the energy to swim or stand. The water,

103

meanwhile, would keep rising, and eventually it would drown the victim. Slowly, painfully, but as surely as one day followed the other.

"We're going to transport you to the hospital, Sarah." The medic leaned in and smiled at her. Behind him someone else was moving a stretcher into the room.

Sarah shook her head and pushed the oxygen mask away from her face. "No! My . . . doctor gave me permission . . . to stay." She stared at them, tired from the effort of talking, and just short of angry. "I have a right . . . to stay; I know what's happening."

A tension hung in the room as the staff members and medical team stopped and stared at her. Our of the corner of her eye Sarah saw Beth quickly leave the room. Sarah coughed twice and waved off the attempts to return the mask to her face. "I'm fine. I need to talk." She drew a few quick breaths and looked each of them in the eyes. "I'm dying; I know that. But I refuse to . . . die in a hospital when this . . . this is my home."

The medic took a step back and looked at his peers.

Just then Beth burst back into the room with what looked like a patient chart. She took hold of the medic's arm, her voice passionate. "She's telling the truth." Beth held the chart up and read the notes written there. "Dr. Cleary listed her as a D.N.R. Do not resuscitate. She's been given permission to die here, without a trip to the hospital as long as her symptoms are caused by heart failure." Beth looked up at the man. "They are, right?"

"She's very sick, ma'am. We only want to give her the best possible care."

Mr. Johnson, the manager on duty, stepped forward. "Let's honor her wishes. We'll keep her on oxygen. If there's anything else we can do, please let us know."

A look of resignation crossed the medic's face. "She could be on intravenous fluids, but as long as she can sip from a straw, the IV isn't absolutely necessary." He lowered his voice. "Her lungs are very wet; to be honest, she may not have more than a few days."

Sarah felt a sense of elation flash through her. She still had a few days! Just like Dr. Cleary had said! And at this point in her life, that was all that mattered, because a few more days was all she needed.

God was giving her enough time to finish telling her story to Beth Baldwin.

CHAPTER ELEVEN

THE GROUP OF PEOPLE standing near Sarah's bed talked for another few minutes but the decision had been made, they would follow the plan outlined in Sarah's chart.

She could stay.

Sarah wanted to shout for joy, but she was too tired. Instead she held out her hand to Beth and mouthed the words, "Thank you."

The others left the room, but Beth stayed. She squeezed Sarah's hand, her eyes watery with tears. "Sarah, I'm . . . I'm sorry. I wish you weren't so sick."

Sarah held tight to Beth's fingers. The medic had removed the oxygen mask and placed two small air tubes into either side of her nose so she could talk. Her words came slower than she would've liked, but at least they came. "Don't be . . . sorry. I'm ready to go." A smile tugged at the corners of her mouth. "I have just . . . one thing left to do."

Beth pulled up a chair and stroked Sarah's hand. Two small tears fell from her eyes and splashed across her cheeks. "Is it what I think?"

"Yes." Sarah hesitated, waiting until she caught her breath. The waters were rising; she could feel them even now. "I must finish the story."

"Finish it today, Sarah." Beth wiped at her cheek. "Please."

"No." A feeling of peace and knowing settled over

Sarah's soul. "Today is the tenth day . . . I will tell you . . . only that part."

Beth exhaled and fearful uncertainty colored her expression. "But what if . . ."

Sarah shook her head. She could feel the light shining in her eyes. "God will give me three days." She pressed her hand against her heart. "I know it in here." She made a gentle motion toward the night-stand. "But I'll need . . . your help, Beth."

Beth bit her lip, her expression determined. "I'm here, Sarah. Whatever you need I'm here."

"Very well." Sarah relaxed against her pillows and found the window once more. "Let's get started."

Beth was filled with dread, and nothing Sarah said about being ready or having three more days did anything to relieve the feeling. In the days of December, she'd come to rely on Sarah in some way she couldn't quite define. In a world turned upside down, a world where divorce and defeat and discouragement reigned, "Sarah's Song" had given her hope again.

And now Sarah was dying.

Even the medics had said so; Sarah Lindeman was going to die, and then what? Who would remember her song or her story? And what if she didn't live long enough to finish it?

The questions haunted her even as Sarah asked her to take the ornament from the tenth envelope. The frail piece of paper inside read *Victory,* and Beth found a place for it on the small tree. Bit by bit, the story began to spill from Sarah's lips in soft breathy bursts.

As it did, Beth felt her anxiety grow dim, felt herself forget about the panic that had been welling up inside her since she'd arrived at work and saw the ambulance and fire truck parked outside.

Sarah's words soothed her soul, allowed her to be carried back, back in time to the fall of 1941, to the next part of the story.

Sarah explained how Trailway Records released "Sarah's Song" as a single and placed it on a fast track. It came out in mid-November, and immediately hit number one on the country charts. Sarah was an overnight sensation.

"You were a celebrity, Sarah!" Beth narrowed her eyes, surprised. One of the girls on staff had mentioned something about Sarah being a professional singer in her day, but a number one single? "No wonder Sam heard the song."

"He didn't . . . hear it right away." Sarah inhaled through her nose and waited a moment. When she'd caught her breath, she picked up the story again.

Offers poured in and dates were set for Sarah to cut her first album. Everywhere she went people congratulated her on her success, praising her voice and the impact the song was making in the lives of the listeners. But it wasn't enough for Sarah.

"Victory would only come if Sam heard the song." She chuckled softly and it became a series of short coughs. "In the end, he didn't hear the song at all, but an interview. A radio interview."

Sam Lindeman had been at home in his New Jersey apartment on Saturday morning, about to enjoy a two-week break from school, when he flipped on the radio. Instantly, he recognized the voice of the woman speaking. It was Sarah; he would know her voice after a hundred years of missing her.

He turned up the volume and heard what she had to say.

Sarah's eyes drew distant. "The announcer asked me what had inspired 'Sarah's Song,' and I told him. I'd loved just one man in my life, and I'd lost him. I would do anything to have him back again, but it was too late. The announcer asked me his name and I told him. Sam. Sam Lindeman. Then I took it a step further. 'Sam,' I said over the air. 'If you're out there, I'm sorry for leaving. I love you; I always will.'"

Sarah's words were slow with frequent stops but that didn't matter. Beth hung onto every line, imagining a young man sitting near the radio, hearing the woman he still loved declaring her feelings for him.

When the interview was over, the station played "Sarah's Song." Sam allowed every word to work its way into his heart. His career gave him little time for listening to music, so that was the first time he'd heard it. But long before the song was over he knew what he had to do.

That afternoon he called the school's superintendent and explained that something had come up; he wouldn't be able to finish out the semester because he had to get home. The next day he packed his things and boarded a train back to South Carolina.

"And that's the tenth part of the story." Sarah closed her eyes for a moment and then blinked them open.

"I'm tired, Beth. Too tired to sing."

Beth's throat felt thick, and she swallowed back her sorrow. "That's okay. You can sing the song tomorrow."

Sarah nodded, but she was already asleep.

That night after she tucked Brianna in, Beth found Bobby sitting in the TV room, the television off. "Hey." She sat down beside him and waited until he looked at her. "I'm sorry if I've been mean these past few weeks."

The lines on his forehead softened. He eased his arm around her shoulders and pulled her close. They stayed that way a long while before he spoke. "I understand. Leaving isn't easy."

She wanted to say something more, something about working things out or finding a way to fall in love again. But she couldn't. Leaving was still the right choice, wasn't it? The only way either of them would ever be happy again?

After a while, they both stood and found their separate sleeping areas.

"Sarah's Song" rang in Beth's mind again that night, especially those four words that had stayed with her. *It's not too late . . . It's not too late . . .*

The next day, she could hardly wait to get to work and find out what happened next—what Sam had done once he arrived back in Greer with his things.

Sarah's breathing was more labored that morning, but her spirits were high. This was the eleventh day of her ritual, which meant she was almost at the end. The prospect gave her an energy she hadn't had since the first day, and it made Beth certain that somehow Sarah was right.

She would live long enough to finish the story.

Not for herself, but for Beth. For whatever was happening in Beth's heart and soul and mind. And because only at the end would she hear the rest of "Sarah's Song" and learn the secret of love.

The secret only Sarah could share.

CHAPTER TWELVE

THE ELEVENTH ORNAMENT read *Embrace,* and again Beth hung it on the tree for Sarah. Only one envelope remained now. When the newest ornament was in its proper place, Sarah drew a slow breath and began.

Sam arrived in Greer on Monday, December 22, and immediately took a cab to Sarah's house. Her parents were thrilled to see him, but they explained that Sarah wasn't there. She was writing again, something she liked to do at Greer Park, on the far bench near the big grassy field.

Sam knew the place; he and Sarah had met there before. He hugged Sarah's parents and headed for the park.

"Actually, I wasn't writing a song that day," Sarah smiled, her eyes suddenly watery. "I was writing in my journal, asking God about Sam. I looked up and—" Her mouth hung open, but she couldn't speak. The soft folds of her chin trembled and a tear made its way down her leathery cheek. She shook her head. "I'm sorry. This is my favorite part." She gazed out the window. "I looked up and there he was. Sam Lindeman, walking toward me. I thought . . . I thought I was seeing things until he walked right up and held out his hands."

Sarah closed her eyes and a smile worked its way up her cheeks. More tears splashed onto her face, but the smile remained. "I can hear him now, see him. Standing there, arms outstretched. I went to him and the feel of his arms . . ." She opened her eyes and looked at Beth. "Has stayed with me a lifetime. I don't need the twelve days or the ornaments to feel his arms around me. I was born for that moment, and the memory of that embrace will stay until I draw my last breath."

Beth swallowed hard and realized there were tears on her own cheeks.

"I'll finish the story tomorrow." Sarah folded her hands, simple and demure.

Reluctantly, Beth bent over and kissed Sarah on the forehead. "I'll be here."

That night, again, Beth's heart felt softer than before. She caught herself making conversation with Bobby, even laughing at something he said. But the morning couldn't come soon enough, and when it did, she hurried to Sarah's room, desperately hoping the woman was still alive.

It was Christmas Eve, the twenty-fourth of December. The Twelfth Day of Christmas. Sarah was awake, gray and tired, but her eyes sparkled. "Are you ready for the rest of the story, Beth?"

She dropped to the chair, and gave Sarah's hand a gentle squeeze. "Yes. Please . . . go ahead."

"Today, the ornament comes last."

"Okay."

Sarah breathed in and coughed several times. Then—in a way that even her failing health couldn't stop—the story came.

That day at the park, Sam held onto her for what felt

113

like forever. When he pulled back he asked her nothing about the past or Nashville or what had happened to bring her home again.

Instead he held out a ring and asked her to be his wife.

"We sat on that park bench," Sarah stared out the window, "the rest of the afternoon. Kissing, talking . . . amazed we'd found each other. Until he died we returned to that bench again and again and again." She closed her eyes and when she opened them, her lashes were damp. "I feel him there, with me, every time I see that old bench. Even now that he's been gone so many years."

Beth nodded. If only Sarah could make it over to the window one more time. Maybe when the story was finished.

Sarah went on, explaining how she and Sam told her parents about their engagement and how her mother pulled her aside. She paused, weary from the effort, but clearly determined to press on.

"My mother gave me something that night. Look under my bed, Beth. Please."

Beth hesitated, but only for a moment. She didn't want to look under the bed; she wanted the story. But Sarah's expression pleaded with her, and Beth nodded. She dropped to her knees and there, under the bed, was a small white box. "This?" She pulled it out and held it up for Sarah to see.

"Yes." Sarah looked at the box as if it were a long lost friend. "Open it. I don't bring it out until the twelfth day."

Beth sat back in her chair and lifted the top from the box, her movements slow and reverent. Inside lay a pair of red gloves, worn and slightly faded. She looked up at Sarah, puzzled. "Your mother gave you gloves?"

"Red gloves." Sarah's eyes sharpened, and a knowing look filled her expression. "I'm giving them to you, Beth. Put them on."

Beth was overcome with a sense of awe. Sarah had obviously cherished the gloves for sixty years, but now . . . now she was giving them away. "Sarah, I can't take—" She stopped when she saw the certainty in Sarah's eyes. "You really want me to have them?"

"Yes." Sarah's eyes glistened.

Beth hesitated, looking down at the gloves. With great care she slid them on, first one hand, then the other.

Only then did she see the white stitching, the embroidery that made a pattern across the palms of both gloves. She was about to ask what it meant when she realized it wasn't a pattern at all, but words.

Her eyes found Sarah. "There's . . . a message here, isn't there?"

"There is." Sarah was teary again. "Hold your hands up toward heaven. That's the only way to read it."

Beth did as she was told, holding her outstretched hands heavenward. As she did, the words sprang to life. The palm of the left red glove read, *Above all else . . .* " And the palm of the right glove read, *"guard your heart."*

Above all else, guard your heart.

Sarah smiled through her tears and made a small shrug with her tired shoulders. "There it is, Beth. The secret of love. Above all else, guard your heart. It's a Bible verse, Proverbs 4:23."

Beth stared at the words and felt them penetrating her soul, probing about and challenging her in a way nothing ever had. "I . . . I've never heard that before."

"You see," Sarah sniffed and adjusted the oxygen tubes in her nose. "If I would've guarded my heart, Beth, I never would've given myself to Mitch Mullins. I would have realized Sam's worth long before I ever left Greer."

Beth stared at the gloves for a long time. "Sarah . . . I can't take these. They're . . . they're too precious. Your children should have them."

"No." Sarah's eyes shone. "God wants you to have them, dear. He told me you need that message this Christmas."

The gloves were soft on her fingers, and Beth held them to her face. They smelled of old love and days gone by, and they were warm. Not so much against her cheeks as they were warm against her heart. "Thank you, Sarah. I'll treasure them."

Eventually she let her hands fall to her lap and she looked at Sarah. "What happened then, with you and Sam?"

"We didn't want to wait, so we got married." She looked toward the window again, lost once more to the past.

The couple gathered their closest friends and

family and the preacher from Greer Community married them on Christmas Eve at the park, right in front of the bench where Sarah had written the song, the place where Sam had found her when he returned to Greer.

"You can open the last envelope now, Beth."

The gloves remained as Beth reached for the envelope and pulled out the final ornament. The word read *Still,* and Beth felt the sting of tears as she placed it on the plastic tree.

"We married on Christmas Eve." Sarah's eyes were dreamy, her smile that of a girl sixty years younger. "I wore a white dress and the red gloves. The ceremony was short, and halfway through it started to snow. Our preacher pronounced us husband and wife and then Sam turned to me and started to sing." She hesitated, still amazed. "He knew all the words."

And then, the way Sam had sung to her that magical Christmas Eve, Sarah began to sing.

" 'It's not too late for faith to find us . . . Not too late for right to win.' " The words came crisp, clear despite Sarah's struggle to breathe. " 'Not too late, let love remind us. Not too late to try again.' "

Sarah closed her eyes, squeezing out two small streams of tears. "I took over from there, singing the entire song to him, all three verses. When I finished, the pastor said he had just one prayer for the two of us. That fifty years from then, we would still know the words to the song, still make time to sing it the way we were singing it that night."

Still.

The word on the twelfth ornament. Beth looked at the tree, at the words scattered amidst the branches. It was the greatest love story Beth had ever heard, but the best part of all was the lesson in the red gloves. *Above all else, guard your heart.*

Sarah lifted her tired hands and pulled them across her cheeks. "I still love him, Beth." Their eyes met. "I still love him, and I still remember the song. Just the way the pastor prayed that Christmas Eve." Sarah settled back some, her eyes never leaving Beth's. "You know why I only remember the details of our story once a year?"

"No." The question had come up several times, but Beth had never voiced it. "How come?"

"Because going back makes me miss him, and—" Her voice cracked, and for the first time since the story's beginning Sarah was overcome with emotion. Sobs shook her, stopping her from speaking and causing her shoulders to shake. The pain in the old woman's face was so gut-wrenching Beth considered calling for help. But then gradually, it began to ease. Her weathered hands came up and covered her face and the sounds of her soft cries filled the room. "God, how I miss him."

Beth stared at her hands, at the red gloves and the message written across the palms. After a while, Sarah stopped crying. She sat a little straighter and exhaled long and slow. "I'll be going home soon; I'm ready now." She smiled through her tears. "Sam's been waiting a long time for me to join him."

There were a hundred things Beth wanted to say,

things she wanted to ask. What happened next, and how long before they had children. How did they keep their love alive and how—after more than six decades—did she still feel the same way about Sam Lindeman.

But Sarah's eyes were closing. "I . . . I'm finished, Beth."

"Sarah, wait . . ." Beth leaned forward and gave Sarah's arm a light shake.

Sarah opened her eyes. Her gaze was so direct, so sincere it took her breath away. "I believe you have something to do, Beth." She hesitated. "It's Christmas Eve. Do it now; before it's too late."

Before Beth could respond, Sarah nodded and fell asleep.

But that was okay, because Sarah was right. Beth had something to do, and nothing was going to stop her. Tucking her gloved hands into her pockets, she slipped downstairs and outside and crossed the street to the park.

She found the bench instantly and the moment she sat down, she started to cry. Her tears came with an intensity similar to Sarah's, but for different reasons. She didn't miss a man long dead, but she'd very nearly missed the truth. If not for Sarah's story, her song, Beth would've walked out on the man God Himself had given her, a love she was suddenly desperate to fight for.

The words embroidered across the palms of the red gloves shouted at her now. She didn't need to talk to Sarah about how she and Sam had kept their love alive. The secret was right there, plain as day.

Above all else, guard your heart.

It was five o'clock when Beth finally got home that evening.

The red gloves still on her hands, she took the bulky package from the back seat of her car and was halfway up the walkway when Bobby opened the door. "Beth, I . . ." He stopped, his mouth open, eyes wide.

In her hands were four dozen yellow roses.

The tears blurred her vision, and she blinked so she could see his reaction. She stopped walking, stood there in the glow of the Christmas Eve moon, and before he could say another word, she started to sing.

"It's not too late for faith to find us. Not too late for right to win." Tears came but she sang anyway. Never mind the freezing night air or the fact that her voice was not smooth and rich like Sarah's. It was sincere. And the words came straight from her heart as she sang them to the man she still loved, the man she almost lost.

"It's not too late, let love remind us. Not too late to try again."

She began walking toward him, her eyes locked on his. "I'm sorry, Bobby." Before she reached the front porch she saw that he, too, was holding something. The smell hit her just as she realized what it was.

A fresh-baked key lime pie.

"Merry Christmas, Beth." His eyes were red and wet as he led her into the house.

A sweet, tart smell warmed the air, and suddenly

Beth realized what she was seeing. There, on every available surface in the kitchen, were key lime pies. She stared at them, and slowly, in a way that would've made old Sarah proud, she set the flowers down and melted into her husband's embrace.

"Don't ever let go, Beth." He whispered the words against her hair, trembling from desire and desperation and the decision they'd almost made to end it all. "Please, don't let go."

Brianna came running into the kitchen, her eyes dancing. "Mommy, guess what? Me and Daddy baked you a hundred pies!" She joined the hug, her little arms tight around both of them.

Beth smiled at their daughter, the feel of Bobby's embrace still warming her from the inside out.

"Ten, to be exact." Bobby met her gaze and looked straight to the center of her heart. "I stopped trying, Beth. I'm sorry." He kissed her, ignoring Brianna's giggles. "I'll never stop again."

For a moment, Beth looked down at the red gloves. Bobby did the same and he made a curious face. "Are those new?"

Beth lifted her hands and framed his face with the furry red wool. "Yes. They're from a good friend."

"It's going to be the bestest Christmas." Brianna jumped up and down as she trailed away from them across the living room. "We have enough pie for a million weeks. Plus tomorrow is Christmas and . . ."

Their daughter's happy voice faded as Beth kissed Bobby, long and slow and with a lifetime of feeling. The way she hadn't kissed him in years.

"I guess . . ." He came up for air and grinned at her. "I guess this means you're not moving out."

Beth worked her gloved fingers through his hair and buried her head into his shoulder. "Not now or ever." She thought about Sarah. "Wait till I tell you what happened."

EPILOGUE

THE IMAGE CAME OUT OF NOWHERE.

Sarah was sitting straight up in bed, struggling to breathe, when suddenly she saw it as clearly as if it were happening there in the room before her. Only there was a problem. Sarah's eyes were closed; she couldn't possibly be seeing people standing before her.

The image was of Beth and a young man and a little girl, locked in an embrace not far from a Christmas tree. They were smiling and the look on their faces said much about the strength of their feelings for each other.

The picture was so strong, she opened her eyes and looked about the room. *God?* She couldn't voice the words so she said them in her head. *Is it true? Are things okay with Beth? Did the story change her?*

The answer resonated deep within her, and she knew what had happened. God had granted her the miracle she'd asked for. He'd allowed her to live long enough to tell her story, to pass on the miracle of "Sarah's Song." And in the process, the love between her and Sam would continue even after they were both dead and forgotten.

Sarah saw the image once more, Beth with her family, and she smiled. Then, in a sudden rush, she realized she could no longer draw a single breath. Again she tried, and again, until she realized what was happening. Her life was draining away, but she felt no urgency, no desire to press the panic button.

It was time to go home, and what better day than Christmas Eve.

The night of the greatest miracle of all.

The service was small, attended by Sarah's children and several grandchildren.

Beth stood at the back next to Bobby, and when it was over, she found her way to Sarah's daughter and introduced herself. "Here." She held out the red gloves. "Your mother gave me these because I needed them."

The woman recognized the gloves immediately, and took them, clearly grateful. "I wondered what happened to them. I found the tree and the ornaments, but not the gloves."

"Yes." Beth nodded. "She thought I needed them, and I did." She glanced back at Bobby and shot him a sad smile over the small crowd. She looked at Sarah's daughter again and sniffed. "I don't need them; I understand the message now." She paused, her throat thick. "I thought you'd want to keep them in the family."

The woman had Sarah's clear blue eyes. She hesitated for a moment. "Did she teach you the song?"

"Yes."

A knowing look dawned in the woman's expression. "Then . . . you're the one."

Beth lowered her brow, confused, and waited for the woman to explain herself.

"Last year at this time, I spent Christmas with Mother. She told me God was going to give her one more year, one more time to go through the twelve days and remember the story she and Dad had shared." Sarah's daughter blinked back tears, her chin quivering. "I asked her why she thought that and she told me someone out there needed a miracle. She was sure that if only that person would listen to the story, the miracle would happen, and a life would be changed forever."

Beth was too choked up to speak. She hugged Sarah's daughter and took a final look at the white casket and the spray of roses that covered it. On the way home she stared out the window. How good was God to give Sarah a reason to live an extra year? To let the miracle be hers, a miracle she had needed more than she'd known?

Suddenly an idea hit her.

She turned to Bobby and grinned. "Hey, let's go home and make something."

He raised an eyebrow and gave her a welcoming smile. "Make something?"

A giggle slipped from her lips and she gave him a playful shove. "Not that, silly." She loved this, the way it felt to be with Bobby now. The two of them had found their way back to the beginning. She had shared Sarah's story with him, and taught him the song. What had happened between them in four short days was beyond explanation, and together they were determined to hold on forever to what they'd found.

Bobby angled his head, his eyes on the road. "Okay, then what should we make?"

"Well . . ." Beth bit her lip, and in the corner of her mind she could almost see Sarah smiling from heaven. "How about a dozen ornaments?"

Center Point Publishing
600 Brooks Road ● PO Box 1
Thorndike ME 04986-0001 USA

(207) 568-3717

US & Canada:
1 800 929-9108

NE

11/01